The Rancher's Reason

Rachel Blanchard

1

For as the heavens are higher than the earth, so are my ways higher
than your ways, and my thoughts than your thoughts.
Isaiah 55:9

"Please, Willow? All my friends volunteer there. I don't want to get
behind on my hours."

Willow Hutchins sighed as her little sister, Aria, gazed at her with
bright blue eyes from across Willow's desk in her chorus room at
Hoffman Haven High. Previously organized choral scores spread out
in heaps on every chair after her ninth graders had swarmed out of
the high-ceilinged room two minutes ago with the bell.

At fourteen, Aria was hardly a baby anymore, but she knew just
what to say to break down Willow's carefully built defenses. "Can't
you earn scholarship hours anywhere else?"

The thought of facing Ace Sterling again made Willow's lunch of
leftover lasagna turn to stone in her stomach.

"No," Aria said immediately. She counted off the objections with
her fingers. "The hospital has too many volunteers, summer camp is
full, and Mrs. Woods said that working at the diner with Mom and
Dad doesn't count since I get paid."

Apart from the way Aria's beautiful, rounded face contrasted
with Willow's narrow, angular one, the two could be mistaken for
twins. Her sister was effortlessly cute and comfortable in gray cotton

sweats and designer sneakers, her raven hair captured by a claw clip, while "Ms. Hutchins," Hoffmann Haven High's new choir teacher, was styled in a way that Aria liked to call a bit "extra."

Plucky yellow chicks sporting rain boots swung at the end of Willow's long dangle earrings, and shimmering pink strands streaked through the weave of her fuzzy, pastel cardigan. It was spring, a time for new beginnings—and apparently—facing past ghosts.

Willow dropped her head into her hands, crinkling the teacher's music score on her cluttered desk. "When would you start?"

Aria shrieked and circled the desk to give Willow a hug. "Thank you! You won't regret this."

Willow pictured Ace's cocky half-smile, and her heart gave a funny little leap. She was pretty sure she would regret this.

"A bunch of kids are headed out there this Saturday. Could you give me a ride? Jordyn would love the horses."

Willow straightened and gripped the desk. "Jordyn is never going to Ernest Ranch."

Aria still thought that Willow's three-year-old daughter was the unexpected blessing born of a poorly-handled rebound relationship. Her sister was unaware that Willow's charming high school sweetheart, Ace Sterling—who also happened to be the co-owner and operator of Sommerton's nearby horse rescue—was Jordyn's father.

Willow's mouth dried up. Ace had no idea he had a daughter, and that had bothered her since Jordyn's birth. Ace'd been so caught up in his old foster dad's dream and had admitted to Willow that he wasn't cut out to be a dad since he'd never had a father figure until his teenage years.

Because of that, Willow felt confident he would never care for them first, the way she needed him to. And even if he was willing to cut back on his ranch time and get married, wouldn't he grow to resent her for asking him to lay down the most important passion of his life?

She'd decided it was easier to separate than to risk a lifetime of chasing him around and competing for his attention. She had the support of family and friends around her, and Jordyn was thriving. Surely Willow wouldn't have to face Ace if she just dropped Aria off in the rescue's parking lot.

"Make sure you send them your seizure care plan," Willow

warned, one finger up.

"I know, I know." Aria slung her bookbag over her shoulder as the bell rang, ending Willow's precious planning time. Aria grinned. "I can't wait to see Ace again."

Aria Hutchins. Ace's stomach had plummeted once her online volunteer application had popped up in his inbox. Instantly, visions of an eager ten-year-old girl had appeared in his mind.

Her wide smile was full of braces. He remembered her tugging his arm, wanting to show him her collection of porcelain ponies, and trying as hard as she could to hang out with her big sister and her boyfriend.

Her big sister—Willow—was someone Ace would rather not see again. When Wyatt Ernest, the only father figure he'd ever known, had been dying, he'd asked Ace to keep his life's work going. As close as Ace and Willow had become while they dated for three years, it still made no sense how she could dump him and then immediately run into someone else's arms.

He'd thought their love would last a lifetime, but instead, he'd been left alone again. He'd made a new home for himself in Sommerton, an old German farming town far enough north to prevent him from ever bumping into Willow Hutchins. Until a familiar red sedan rolled down Ernest Ranch's dirt drive.

Ace had hoped Patrick or Riley Hutchins would drop Aria off for her volunteer shift, but here Willow was, her eyes wide as she saw him propped against his poop shovel in the parking lot. This was not the way he'd hoped to see her again, four years later. Oh well, he'd look like a coward if he ran away now. Instead, Ace leaned back against the chipped metal railing of the paddock and tipped his hat.

Willow was even more stunning than Ace had remembered, with that dark hair, smattering of freckles across her nose, and welcoming glint in her blue eyes, as if she had no idea that she was, in fact, the most beautiful woman in the world. He'd been wise, very wise, to keep his distance all this time. Despite his casual posture, she still had the power to shake him up.

Thankfully, he didn't have much time to focus on his former flame, because Aria leapt out of the passenger seat and called out, "Ace!"

He embraced her with his free arm and chuckled. "Hey, kiddo.

Don't get too close, I'm doing a dirty job here."

"That's okay, I came prepared." Aria sashayed back and forth, showing off her braid, plaid button-up shirt and dark-wash jeans. The clothes looked brand new and too nice to labor in, but he didn't want to discourage her on her first day.

"Perfect. I can't believe how grown up you are. How've things been?"

"Great."

Ace's brow furrowed. "I saw in that email you've got epilepsy now?"

Aria huffed. "I'm fine, it was just one seizure. They've controlled it with medicine, but we had to let you know just in case."

"Well, I'm glad you're doing all right now." He adjusted the shovel as Willow, still in the car, lowered the window exactly two inches.

She looked at Ace for only a split second. "Hello. Have a great first day, Ari."

"Aren't you going to come out?" Aria asked her.

Ace shuffled his feet and bit back a smile. Aria might've grown up, but she hadn't lost her precocious nature.

Willow's cheeks flushed. So, she was still highly susceptible to teasing. "Sorry, I have an appointment to get to," she said. "You're welcome for the ride."

Aria whispered to Ace, "I'd better let her go now, or she won't come back to get me." She waved cheerily and called, "Bye, sis!"

Willow's car screeched forward toward the paddock before she corrected and reversed. Interesting. She was as flustered by seeing him again as he was seeing her.

Aria planted her hands on either side of her sparkling belt. "So boss, what are we going to do first?"

"I'll let you pick. We're selling pails of carrots here," Ace gestured to a plastic table by the front gate, "that people can feed to the horses, or you could learn to lead the pony rides."

"Definitely the ponies!"

"I figured as much." They walked into the ranch. "Did you read anything about what we do here?"

"This is like a retirement home for horses, right?"

"Pretty much. We've got some regular celebrities here. A former

4

show horse, Wyatt's horse, the mascot of Ernest Farm, and an old racer. Then we have two we're boarding for their owners, and unfortunately, a brother and a sister pony we rescued whose owners couldn't afford to take care of them anymore."

The Shetlands ponies had been left behind after things got rough and the caretaker had second thoughts. Ace knew how that felt.

But now he was ending abandonment and making things right. He'd found his life's purpose. Hopefully, he could afford to continue to carry it out. He'd give everything he had to try.

Aria quickened her step once they approached the twin blue stables. Sure, the buildings could use a fresh coat of paint, but a wave of satisfaction washed over Ace as he saw her delight at seeing the majestic animals. Another reason he loved doing what he did.

"Howdy, Cowboy."

Ace spun at the too-familiar voice. He took in the starched collar that was completely inappropriate attire for a ranch, and two beady eyes set under gelled-back ginger hair. Dan Achan.

Ace pasted on a cordial smile. "Good morning, Dan. I'm showing my newest helper around. Why don't you head outside my office to wait while I get her settled? It will only take a minute."

Dan stepped towards him, and when Ace squared up so that the shorter man's head merely reached his chin, Dan stepped right back again. "When are you going to sell me this ranch, Sterling? I know you're hurting for money."

Dan was hurting for a swift punch in the nose. "You know I'm not interested."

"Will Ernest is, and he let it slip that your veterinary bills have stacked up mighty high this year."

"Will isn't going to sell to you, either." Ace's foster brother may be busy with his law career, but Will wouldn't backstab him like that. Even if he was upset that the loan he'd provided to keep the ranch running had been poured into this place, with no returns in sight.

"Will won't sell, until you stop digging your heels in the mud."

It might have been unprofessional of Ace, but he slapped his hand on his right knee and ground his boot down good.

Dan threw his hands up in the air. "Just remember. My offer still stands, for now. You may make me so mad one of these days that I just snatch it away."

"Then I guess you and your fancy set of cookie-cutter, clapboard houses will have to be disappointed."

Dan stormed away. Good riddance. Ace turned to an open-mouthed Aria. "Sorry about him."

"Oh, I've heard all about Dan from my parents. He's always causing trouble at their Chamber of Commerce meetings."

Dan already managed two luxury apartment complexes in Hoffman Haven. The additions had clogged up traffic and diminished the small town's historic charm. Now, he had his sights set on Sommerton—specifically, Will and Ace's fifty acres of sparkling streams and rolling hills, conveniently located just twenty minutes outside of St. Louis.

Aria tucked a dark strand of stray hair behind her ear. "Is it true what he said? Is the ranch in trouble?"

"We've had better days financially. But that's not something for you to worry about. God will provide. This is a good cause, and we'll figure something out."

Aria nodded, but she didn't look convinced.

The morning carried a cool April breeze, but the relentless sun combined with Dan's intrusion were making Ace sweat. He fanned himself with his hat. "How are Patrick and Riley?"

"Oh, the same. Except Mom fills her days with babysitting Jordyn now and spoils her terribly."

Ace clamped his lips together. He'd heard that Willow had had a child in college but that the baby's dad had left her early on. He hated to think of Willow being hurt like that, but she'd been the one to kick Ace out of her life. He couldn't go back, not when she clearly wanted nothing to do with him.

Still, every time he'd thought about dating someone else, he just couldn't follow through. He'd fallen for Willow hard. He guessed he was slow to love, but slow to recover once he had loved. It was hard to picture starting over with another person.

Aria smirked. "Willow will be glad to hear you haven't cut your curls off."

Ace promptly shoved his hat back down, clear over his ears. "I've been too busy to get to the barber." He always thought his golden ringlets made him look too much like a princess, but Willow loved them and had convinced him to stop buzzing his hair. He'd forgotten how many little things about him she'd had a hand in. "And how's your sister been?"

"Lonely." Aria shook her head. "She works too hard. She's actually my choir director now."

"I can just see that." Ace was glad to hear Willow had finished college. She was always at the top of every class they'd taken together.

School wasn't really Ace's thing, but he'd admired how much she loved to study and create, especially in her music classes. Willow's sweet voice could make a man forget about all his problems for one song and then confess his feelings in the next. Of course, music was in her blood.

"Is your dad still playing fiddle at the diner on Friday nights?" Ace asked.

"Of course. He gets Willow to join him on the mic sometimes."

"That's nice." He refused to contemplate how much he'd enjoyed hearing her sing and how much he missed it.

"Hey, Aria." Bo Ernest led Inky by the reins to the paddock as the first visitors of the day began to filter in.

"Hey, Bo. I didn't know you'd be here." Ace noticed that Aria seemed nervous.

"This was my grandad's ranch." Bo rubbed Inky's nose.

"Oh. Right."

My land, Ace had forgotten the social awkwardness of teenagers. "Bo here is my second hand. Couldn't keep this place running without him. Can you show Aria how to lead the pony rides? I've got paperwork to do."

"Sure."

"Stay right by her the first couple rounds, until she gets to feeling comfortable."

"Okay, then." Aria followed after Bo, and Ace gave her a thumbs up.

Ace missed the days when he'd just spend time with the horses and the guests, but right now, there were more grants to be written. More red-stamped envelopes to file, along with his returned requests for payment extensions. He'd kept his job down at the train station during the week, but it hadn't been enough. If something didn't turn around soon, Ace feared Aria's first day on the job may not be too far from her last.

"Umm..." a familiar soprano sound made Ace spin on his heels to find Willow with one arm fully extended before her, awkwardly dangling a floral lunch bag from her slender fingers.

He looked at Willow in astonishment.

She cleared her throat. "Aria forgot her lunch."

"Oh," he said intelligently. He took the lunch bag by its base. "Thank you."

"No, thank you." She smiled. Her lips were lacquered with a rosy, glittery sheen. "Well, see you around."

"See ya." Ace tipped his hat again, wondering if she'd noticed his curls like Aria had.

He hoped he and Willow wouldn't run into each other much. She still had an effect on him, that much was clear. An effect that he couldn't afford to feel again.

He needed to concentrate on saving the ranch. He'd try to stay away from the parking lot on Saturdays from now on. Far away from all the memories and the pain of a shattered heart.

2

"We have to help him!" Aria clutched the center console of Willow's car as if she were dangling on a rocky precipice, and it was her only handhold.

But Willow would remain firm. The distance she'd created from Ace was the only thing keeping her from falling into her own perilous canyon.

"I promise you, Ace does not want my help. Even if there was something we could do."

"So, you're cool with all those horses being sold off to who knows where?"

Willow carefully navigated the car around the curves of the country road which led to Sommerton. If only she could just as skillfully navigate Aria away from this topic. "When are you getting your driver's license again?"

"A year from now." Aria leaned against her headrest. "Thanks for driving me. It's a little less embarrassing to be dropped off by your sister than by your parents."

Willow shook her head. "Gee, thanks."

Aria grinned. "It's only embarrassing when you forget how to work the gear shift."

"Aria!" Her sister was something else, but she was right on one account. Willow's senses went on high alert the moment the paved road turned into gravel, and their tires bounced over potholes and into Ace's parking lot. Thank goodness, the rancher was nowhere to be found this time.

"Goodbye, troublemaker." Willow twinged Aria's arm lovingly as her sister left. Aria was a good girl, and Willow still worried over her any time she tried something new.

It was great that Aria loved working at the ranch, but she had to stop pushing Willow to volunteer alongside her. Willow had enough to manage without adding on appointments with her ex-boyfriend.

Especially an ex-boyfriend whose honey-colored eyes still set her heart ablaze and whose crooked smile made her doubt her decision four years ago. No, she needed to bury those regrets in the dirt of Ace's passion project, where they belonged.

They had both made the right choice. Willow had her sweet baby girl, and Ace had his horses. Even if a sickly twinge appeared in her stomach at the thought that he might not have them for long.

"Good mornin'." Ace swung a white plastic bucket toward Aria. "Do you want to help me feed the horses?"

"Sounds good!"

Ace walked her to the stables, starting with Sammy. "This stubborn old paint horse used to be your sister's favorite," he mused aloud. He quickly grabbed a carrot to feed to the rascal, who gobbled it up, then shook his mane and pawed the ground for more.

Aria snatched the tidbit up. "Willow liked to come here?"

Why did he have to go and bring up Willow? "Aw, she would pretend like she was no good at riding, and she didn't like to get dirty. I think the horses made her happy, though. Animals are good for a person. Helps them to relax a bit."

"Yes, she needs to breathe more. She's always planning lessons or cleaning the house." Aria's nose wrinkled. "Just maybe don't breathe the air out here."

Did the ranch stink? Ace guessed he had gotten used to it. "Sorry, if it was all a bed of roses, I don't suppose anyone would give you credit for being here." He smirked as he noticed Bo quietly bring his own bucket by theirs to start on the next set of stalls.

Aria shrugged and took out a massive head of lettuce to feed Arrow with. The horse's teeth slid off the end of the leaves.

"Slow down, now. One piece at a time would be better."

Aria's bucket clattered to the ground, the contents spilling out, and time slowed down as the young girl fell backwards. On instinct, Ace slid his arms underneath her just in time. He broke her fall, and possibly his tailbone. He laid her carefully on the ground and frantically looked into her open, glassy eyes.

His brain scrambled for a possible explanation. It landed on the memory of her medical intake form. "Bo, call 911. Aria's having a seizure. Then call Willow back here. Her number is on the clipboard on my desk where I keep the volunteers' emergency contacts." The young man froze, looking as white as Aria. "Go!" Finally, Bo tore off toward the office.

Aria's body jerked forcefully on the dirt, and Ace willed himself to recall her action plan. Was she breathing? Yes. Put her on her side. Loosen her collar. "You're going to be okay," he told the colorless girl. "You're going to be okay. Stay with me, kiddo." He glanced at the time on his watch in case the doctors asked. *Lord, please don't let this last long. Please take care of her.*

Church was another thing that had died with his relationship with Willow, but his relationship with God he'd tried to hold onto. He oftentimes prayed under the vast sky or sweeping trees. He cried out now, *Lord, help. Don't stop listening.*

Willow must have hightailed it back to the ranch, because she rushed over at the same time as a pair of paramedics hopped out of an ambulance with a stretcher.

"Aria!" Willow fell to her knees beside her sister.

"Willow?" Aria asked drearily.

"She's awake. God be praised." Willow clasped Aria's hand.

"Is this the first time she's spoken?" the paramedic asked. She was an elderly woman, with her silver hair swept back into a ponytail.

"Yes, the first time in a minute," Ace answered after a glance down at his watch.

"Did she sustain any injuries that you could see?"

"I don't think so. I caught her head before she hit the ground." Though Ari was conscious, Ace couldn't stop his hands from shaking.

The EMTs lifted Aria and strapped her to the stretcher, even as she protested, "I'm okay now."

"What happened, sweetheart?" Willow leapt into the ambulance after her, and Ace rose as well. "You've been taking your medicine."

"I might've been up too late studying." Aria closed her eyes. Poor kid, having to suffer this because of such an innocent mistake.

"I'm sure she'll be okay now," the uniformed woman told Willow, "but just in case, we're going to get her hooked up with an EEG." Panic splayed over both girls' faces.

"Do you need me to come with you?" Ace asked Willow.

Willow's eyes shone with tears as she peeked out of the open door. "No, but thank you. Thank you so much for being there for her."

The only thing Ace could think of to say to that was, "I love her too, Willow."

For the first time since they reunited yesterday, Willow studied his face. He wondered what she saw there. It must have been positive, because she told him, "I'll call you to let you know what the doctor says."

"I'd appreciate that." His stomach twisted as the paramedic latched Aria's stretcher into place.

"Is your number still the same?"

She'd kept his number? "You know I don't like change." Ace got a smile out of her for that. He watched helplessly as the medical staff shut the two sisters into the ambulance and sped away.

3

Willow called Ace back a little after seven p.m. A cold sweat broke out across her body as soon as she hit the green button to dial, but she had promised to give him an update. She'd known he was a night owl and would be up even after she put Jordyn down for the night.

He picked up after the second ring. "Hello?" Ace's soft baritone greeting sent her heart racing.

"Hi." She launched into explanation. "Aria's doing fine, and Mom and Dad are going to be more vigilant about making sure she goes to bed on time."

"So, she'll still be coming by on Saturdays?"

"She's been cleared to resume all normal activities."

"Good. I'd hate for her to have to stop working with the horses when she'd just started."

Silence hung between them like a stifling blanket. Breathe in, breathe out. It was time for Willow to put aside her pride.

She owed Ace everything for being there for Aria today. If she had hit her head, or fallen down where no one could see her, who knows what could have happened?

"Aria told me she's worried about the ranch closing down."

"We are not closing down." Ace's reply was stern. Terse.

Willow traced the edges of her phone with her thumb. "Then, you're not having financial issues?"

Ace sputtered. "Sure, times are hard. People aren't giving as much as they used to. But I've invested in social media ads to help spread the word about our riding lessons. I'm sure things will turn around soon."

"What kinds of ads? Posts?"

"Well, yeah. We put a picture of Major on a real nice flyer."

Willow shook her head. "Aria can make weekly videos for you. Text and photos don't perform as well anymore. And is that your only source of revenue, riding lessons?"

"We have our petting zoo and pony rides on Saturdays. We have a grant." Ace sounded defensive. Then, he sighed. "I try to fix what I can around the ranch, but the vet bills are killer."

"Have you ever thought about hosting seasonal events? I take..." Willow was about to say she took Jordyn to different activities all the time, but instead, she finished, "I've heard those can be popular."

"I don't know, I'm not good with all that party stuff. You think hosting more events could make that big of a difference?"

"I do." Willow swallowed hard. "Why don't you swing by the diner tomorrow night around five, and we can write up some plans?"

"Oh, I... uh...I guess I'm not doing anything tomorrow night."

He didn't sound enthusiastic about coming, but if she really wanted to pay him back, she'd have to pitch him some stellar ideas instead of taking the easy way out and accepting these fibs that things were going just fine. She'd try this once, and if he didn't take any of her suggestions after that, so be it.

Sunday afternoon, Ace checked on the horses, making sure they had everything they needed. He prayed to God that it was the right move meeting with Willow this afternoon and felt a calming peace coat over the unease he'd been feeling.

He'd bet she was at Hoffmann Haven Church right now, cleaning up the congregation's weekly family-style buffet. He missed the hustle and bustle of well-meaning old ladies and their fine-suited gentlemen, but he hadn't attended a single service since Willow'd broken it off with him.

No one would believe sweet, perfect Willow was to blame for them falling apart. Some of the churchgoers had held her on her first ever Sunday, in a green gingham dress as a newborn baby. He'd seen the pictures.

The men and women of the church had been welcoming when Ace started to attend with Willow in high school, and some had even called him once he'd stopped coming, but he couldn't go back there. That was Willow's church. Willow's town. And Ace was no longer Willow's man.

Ace drove his pickup home to take a shower, his knuckles white on the steering wheel because of all these thoughts resurfacing, when he'd kept them safely bottled up for years. He should have thrown on an old t-shirt, but instead he chose a teal polo picked out by Willow herself.

It hugged his muscles tightly and made him look like less of a schlub. This would be a business meeting, that was all. It was normal to dress up for a business meeting, right?

It was kind of Willow to offer help, and help, he surely needed. But God had a funny sense of humor, to send Ace running back to the woman who'd marked and prodded his heart like she wielded a hot cattle brand.

By muscle memory, Ace found himself under a bright yellow awning with the script "Golden Days Diner" printed on it. He'd found the last parking spot in the lot. When Ace swung open the glass door, peppy music from the 1950s blasted him with a wave of nostalgia.

Black and white posters of movie stars and crooners hung from every corner of the mustard-colored walls, and neon signs brought pops of purple and blue, "for contrast," the Hutchins girls used to say. The booths, chairs, and floor were checkered black and white.

"Ace!" Aria ran toward him, a pencil and order book sticking out of the front pocket of her apron. "Willow's been waiting for you."

Ace pulled her in for a hug. "I'm five minutes early."

Aria rolled her eyes. "You know Willow. She got her spreadsheets open a long time ago. Are you guys preparing for a war or something?"

"Or something." Ace pictured Dan Achan, twirling his mustache like an old Western villain.

Seeing Aria healthy and well again put a spring back in Ace's step, and he strode over to sit across from Willow in a cozy booth. He was careful to back all the way against the back of the seat so their knees wouldn't accidentally brush underneath the table. How different this was from the last time they were here, sipping one milkshake with two straws.

Willow looked up from her laptop with the royal blue cover. "You're here. Finally."

Finally? How dare he be a mere five minutes early.

Aria gave him a sympathetic smile. "What do you want to drink, Ace? Cola?"

He'd actually switched to just water, but Aria looked so pleased to have remembered his favorite drink that he nodded his head. Anyway, Ace might need a pick-me-up if he was to keep up during his and Willow's "war conference."

For a moment, he admired the way Willow's thick hair was swept halfway off her face. The other half was brushed over her collarbones, resting on a bright orange tank top with ribbons as the straps. Her dark lashes squinted in concentration. She took a long sip of her water with lemon and spun her laptop around, so that Ace could see a colorful graphic with Easter bonnets superimposed onto his horses' heads.

He'd planned to be open-minded tonight, but this was just too much. He burst out, "You've got to be kidding me."

Willow held a finger up. "Your events are great, but they haven't been making enough money. Trust me, people want to make special memories with their families, forget about their troubles for a day. They can go see animals almost anywhere. We have to give them a real story, one that fits what they're already looking for."

Ace lowered his head into his hands, realizing his curls were still a little damp from his shower.

"And this month's story...is an Easter Extravaganza!" She drummed her fingers on the lacquered table. "We can decorate the horses' stalls for photo ops, run an Easter egg hunt, set up a dyeing and craft station on the picnic tables..."

"And who's going to pay for all that?"

Willow tossed her hand. "Oh, it won't be much at all. $100 tops. I'll even pick up everything up for you. You know the craft store is my second home."

"And who's going to run this extravaganza?"

"You and your volunteers, of course. I'll put the word out with my students about what we're doing. Once a couple of them decide it would be cool to go, they'll be all in. Which reminds me..." She swiveled the laptop back to pull up a second flyer to show him.

"Ernest Farm is now offering baked goods and horse-themed bracelets in their charming country store!" She paused for effect. "Now I can already see those dollar signs in your eyes, but let me tell you, my chorus girls make bracelets for fun anytime we have a free day. If I let them make bracelets for charity twenty minutes every Friday instead of rehearsing, you'll have enough to sell for the whole year."

Patrick Hutchins appeared behind his daughter, carrying a hefty tray of food. He distributed the plates to the patrons in the next booth over, and then added, "I'm donating the burgers for lunchtime the next couple Saturdays, and Riley and Aria will take care of the treats."

"Patrick, that's too much."

"Please, Son. After the amount of times you came over here, fixing the garbage disposal, repainting, caulking for free? Just try and stop me."

Ace stood to shake his hand. "Thank you. How've you been?"

"Trying to keep all my girls happy. It's not easy, but I do the best I can."

"Dad." Willow crossed her arms, and she looked seventeen again.

"Only kidding."

"Grandpa?" a tiny voice said.

Patrick pivoted. "Here's another of my girls now. Ace, have you met Jordyn?" Patrick laid down his tray and swept up a pint-sized princess with a hundred curls the color of freshly-cut wheat stalks. Her eyes matched Willow's piercing blue shade.

Ace regarded Willow, who turned beet-red. What, did she think that he would be mean to her kid or something?

"Hi, Jordyn, it's nice to meet you."

Jordyn shied away, into her grandfather's chest, but peeked back out with one inquisitive eye.

"Mama's almost done, sweetheart. Why don't you go help Grandpa check the orders while I finish up?" Willow's eyes shone with tenderness toward the child.

Jordyn nodded bravely, and Patrick bounced her back toward the kitchen, singing a showtune all the way.

It felt so strange to be here with the people Ace once thought would be his family. It brought to attention the realization that emptiness had never left him. He just remembered it less out in the country, in the open air. He pulled at the collar of his shirt.

"So, what do you think? Did I convince you?" The hopeful twinkle in Willow's eye cut him straight to the core. How could he refuse her? She had a way of making him believe that good things could happen.

"All right. We'll try it your way this month."

Willow shrieked and clapped her hands. "You won't be sorry."

Ace hoped not. Then again, she'd said that once before.

4

The morning of the Easter Extravaganza, Ace was sitting on the top rung of the rusty paddock when Willow and Aria pulled up. To his surprise, Willow left the car this time.

She huffed. "My mother, who is also my babysitter, mysteriously made a last-minute dentist appointment today, so we've got an extra helper." She opened the back door, and Ace heard the click of a seatbelt unbuckling. Willow swooped Jordyn out of the vehicle as Aria unloaded a gigantic plastic tub from the trunk.

"I'll get that." Ace leapt down and hefted the tub into his arms. "What's in here, cinderblocks?"

"Only the necessary supplies to dress this place up a little," Willow sniffed.

"Look, Mommy, a horsey!" Jordyn pointed to Pinky, who was lazing about the paddock.

"Yes, we get to see horsies today." Willow laid a kiss on Jordyn's chubby cheek. Jordyn crinkled her eyes, grinned a close-lipped smile, and Ace's heart felt like a wrung-out dishcloth.

"Where do you want the bins?" he asked.

"On the picnic benches, please." Willow lowered Jordyn to the ground and captured her hand. Jordyn followed her mother to the wooden seat, her tennis shoes lighting up with every eager step.

Even though having Jordyn along wasn't part of Willow's plan, Ace appreciated how Willow included her in everything, from spreading white linens over the grainy tables, to unwinding sheer lavender fabric and bunching it to make it look decorative down the table's center. Willow applauded every clumsy effort as if it were a grand success, and Ace recalled that was how Willow made everyone feel. Accomplished. Acknowledged. That was what was so intoxicating about being around her.

Ace'd been known as a no-good troublemaker in the back of every class, but when they were paired up for a group project (no doubt by their teacher thinking he needed a positive influence), Willow never treated him with anything less than respect, though she got stern until he started doing his share of the work. She was a natural-born teacher.

He'd been flummoxed by her beauty, but amazingly, she'd developed a crush on him too and had said yes when he asked her to the homecoming dance. He held her close for the first slow song, and thought, what with Wyatt Ernest as his guardian and Willow as his girl, things were finally turning around for him. But then, his life had turned into an excruciating uphill climb, one that he continued to tackle alone.

He chastened himself for that thought that kept rising in him more and more as of late. He'd learned from his short time at church that he had never been alone, even in his childhood, though at times it felt that way. One Bible verse the preacher read struck him to his core: "When my father and my mother forsake me, then the Lord will take me up."

If anyone should have stood by him, it was his parents, but they chose substances over him. Ace wasn't angry about it anymore. Just sad that drugs had such a hold on them that they lost sight of everything that was truly important.

If he had a family, Ace didn't think he could ever do what they did. But it was safer not even to test out his strength, at the risk of continuing a cycle of pain and loss.

That was where the rift with Willow had started. Ace had to go and open his fool mouth and be honest about his lack of hope for ever raising a family. It had seemed like the right thing to do.

He should have known Willow would always be a family-oriented girl. It was a gift she'd been given since birth, a gift he was glad she'd been granted. It had been selfish, really, to keep spending time with her and stealing kisses when they never had a real chance at lasting.

"Ace? Are you okay?" Willow asked, poking his shoulder with a Styrofoam Easter egg.

"Yeah." He shook the cobwebs out to pay more attention to what these girls were doing to his ranch. "Wait, why are you putting those fancy tablecloths up? I thought the kids were supposed to dye eggs?"

"Well..." she hemmed, "I thought it would be much more fun to have a tea party!"

"Willow," Ace growled. "You said this wouldn't cost me much."

"These are all from home, I promise. It's my clearance hoard from last season."

Aria unloaded a curlicue-patterned china tea set, carefully bubble-wrapped in one of the bins.

"Are little kids going to keep this stuff nice?" Ace asked, doubtful. Tea parties were way out of his area of expertise, and he still didn't understand how such a fancy event went along with horses.

Willow tossed her long hair over her shoulders. It was styled in big curls today. "You'd be surprised."

Aria answered, "We can always bleach the cloths if the kids spill. They like to feel grown-up once in a while."

"You two sure are a pair." Forget teaching. They could start their own party planning business.

"You're just lucky we didn't make you dress up as the easter bunny." Willow smirked at Aria.

"Can I help?" Bo had arrived. He'd slicked back the chestnut hair that was usually falling over his eyes. Ace had a guess as to why.

"Know any good places to hide eggs?" Aria lifted two green baskets full.

Ace visualized stinking, melted messes all over the rescue. "I hope those aren't real eggs. Or chocolate."

"Relax, Ace, we filled them with jelly beans. These babies will last all year. Not that we're going to leave them lying around. We'll remember where each one is. Promise." Aria held her palm solemnly in the air and Ace waved her on.

Willow opened up the lid to a glass cake pan. "Lemon bar?" she asked. "They used to make you less cranky."

"I'm not cranky." His tone came out whiny, betraying him. Great.

But Willow's innocent expression and coy smile always broke down his resistance. She didn't mean any harm. Even her hardest teasing couldn't compare to the way he'd been talked to by some of his different foster parents. And she always would apologize if she'd done something wrong.

He'd learned a lot from Wyatt Ernest, but from Willow, Patrick, and Riley as well. Even with all the hurt that Willow had caused by breaking up with him and having a child with someone else, he had to acknowledge that much.

"I'll take a lemon bar." Ace glanced down at his dirt-crusted hands, but Willow magicked up hand sanitizer and a flowered napkin in no time.

"Can I have one?" Jordyn asked. She clasped her hands in front of her and swayed, the universal sign of begging.

"All right."

Willow got one out for herself, too, and they munched on the tangy, sweet snacks.

"That's good." Jordyn licked the last bit of powdered sugar off her palm and wiggled in place.

Ace crossed his arms. "Are you a performer like your mama?"

"Hmm?" she asked.

"Do you like to dance and sing?" rephrased Willow.

"Mm-hmm." Jordyn stuck her chin forward and put her thumb and index finger in the air. "Baby shark, do do do do do do..." Every time she said shark, she punctuated the word by shouting and punching with her other fist until she nearly spun around. It was hilarious, even though the exhibition featured the world's most annoying song.

"She's a natural," Ace agreed. "What other songs do you know?"

"Can we do 'Ring Around the Rosy?'" Jordyn asked.

"No, honey, grown-ups don't like playing 'Ring Around the Rosy,'" Willow replied.

Jordyn stuck out her bottom lip and Ace said, "Speak for yourself." He took her hands, marveling that fingers could be so tiny, and they spun around and around.

When they "all fell down," Ace exaggerated his collapse, putting his big boots up in the air, and was rewarded with a cascade of giggles.

"Again!" she cried. But Willow snatched Jordyn up, tears in her eyes. Ace sat up straight.

"I'm sorry, we have to go now. Aria will help with the party. I hope it goes well."

Willow practically sprinted to the parking lot. Ace let her go, not sure whether she wanted him to follow after. What had he done this time?

On the way home, tears blurred Willow's view as the gravel road transformed back into winding pavement. She tried to hold herself together, but all she could think about was that four years ago, she had made a huge mistake.

She'd told herself then that Ace couldn't be the father and husband she needed, not because she didn't believe he was capable, but because he said himself that he wasn't interested in having his own family. He was only interested in preserving Ernest Ranch, a legacy from the only family he'd ever known.

Seeing Ace with Jordyn today had opened Willow's eyes to the future that she had slammed the door on. A future with two pairs of arms to hold her daughter and two voices to tell her she was loved. Willow had been scared, and she and Ace weren't seeing eye to eye at the time, so she had lied to everyone about Jordyn's parentage. How could she ever tell Ace the truth now?

Willow's cries slipped out audibly, and she pulled to the side of the road.

"Okay, Mommy?" Jordyn asked.

Willow swiped at her eyes and drew in a deep breath.

"Yes, love."

"Don't cry, Mommy."

Willow laughed through her tears at her precious girl. Everything was so simple to Jordyn. "Okay."

Willow's phone on the passenger seat lit up then with a call from her mom. Willow was tempted to ignore it and keep pretending that everything was fine, but she felt a heart nudge, like maybe God sent her a friend to talk to in this moment.

She grabbed the phone, stepped out of the car to the side of the road so Jordyn wouldn't overhear, and picked up the call as she watched her daughter play with her dolls through the backseat window.

"Hello?" Willow's voice warbled.

"What's wrong?"

"Ace is..." Willow started, but a pit of shame opened up in her chest. She couldn't form the rest of the words.

"Is Jordyn's father," Riley finished.

"What? You knew?"

"Why do you think I made up that last minute appointment today? It's about time you got back out there."

Willow groaned. "Mom."

"Jordyn looks just like him. I didn't want to embarrass you since you didn't want to tell anyone, but I knew you didn't have some rebound fling. What I don't understand is why you didn't want to tell anyone. I don't think Ace is the kind of man to take off."

"I don't think so either, but I also don't want someone to feel obligated to stay with me. I want someone to choose to stay with me and Jordyn because he loves us."

"He does love you, sweetheart. And you didn't give him much chance to love Jordyn."

"You mean he *did* love me."

Her mother's New Englander boldness came through again. "I said what I said."

Willow rolled her eyes. Her mom, always the romantic. Willow was sure any soft feelings Ace held for her were gone. Or would be as soon as he knew the truth. "What is he going to think about me now, knowing that kept his own daughter from him all this time?"

"Only God knows. But you chose this path, and you're going to have to live with the consequences. Have some faith that you and Ace can figure this out together."

"But what if we don't?"

"What if you do?" Riley reiterated. "And you know your father and I will be here for you, no matter what."

"Thank you," Willow whispered. "I love you."

"I love you, too. Do you need anything right now?"

"Can you pick Ari up around 2? I'd rather collect myself before facing Ace again."

"Sure."

"Thanks. I'll talk to you tomorrow."

"Bye, hon."

Willow disconnected the call and brushed her hair back, so she wouldn't look messy in front of Jordyn. She'd talk to Ace. Soon.

5

The next Saturday, Willow led Jordyn to a booth at Golden Days, expecting her dad to bring her usual breakfast order of two eggs over medium, hashbrowns, bacon, and a fruit cup. Instead, he slid a gigantic stack of confetti pancakes to Willow's place at the table, complete with sprinkles and whipped topping spelling out, "Happy Birthday, Willow!"

She had to laugh. "Dad, I think these are for Jordyn."

Patrick put down a smaller stack of birthday pancakes for her daughter, who cheered. "Oh no, they're not. I couldn't forget your special day."

"Thanks." She snapped a photo and then cut into the speckled tower.

Riley slid into the booth next to Jordyn and gave her granddaughter a quick squeeze. "And that's not all. We reserved a trail ride for you two hours from now at Ernest Ranch. I'll take care of the babysitting!"

"Mom." Willow's tone was a low warning.

Aria appeared behind her father. "You can't say no to a gift. That's rude. Plus, it will make up for you running out on Ace the other day."

The night of the Easter Extravaganza, Willow had blamed her odd behavior on maternal protectiveness, which could be construed as truth. She did burst into tears because she'd been protective of Jordyn. She simply hadn't mentioned to Aria that the vigilance leading to her outburst had started with a secret four years ago.

Willow gripped her fork. "I hate when you guys gang up on me."

A trail ride at Ernest Ranch for her seventeenth birthday had once been the best gift she'd ever had. Ace made rasta pasta and strawberry cake—her favorite dinner—and they'd enjoyed the beauty of nature and the company of each other. Willow didn't want to hurt her family's feelings, but how awkward would a guided horse ride be now?

"I made the arrangements. Ace made sure he'd be available to take you himself." Aria waggled her eyebrows at Willow. "Don't worry. I'll help you get ready."

"As long as you remember we're just riding horses. I'll throw on some jeans."

"And that hot pink blouse with the frilly sleeves. That would be super cute!"

"You mean the one you 'borrowed' that I haven't seen since last spring?" Willow bit her lip. "I don't know."

"It would be cute and practical." Aria tried a new approach. "It's getting warmer out."

Willow still had her cowgirl boots stored in Aria's closet from her high school days, and after finishing her sugary confection, she followed Aria and Jordyn upstairs to Mom and Dad's apartment above the diner so that she could get ready.

At her sister's white vanity, Willow took extra care with her makeup—though she'd never admit that to Aria—while Ari French-braided the left side of her hair into a pretty ponytail.

Then, Willow spritzed the orange blossom perfume she'd bought at the farmer's market over her top, and she was ready. At least on the outside. On the inside, her heart was skittering from side to side like a newborn colt.

"Mommy, you look like a princess," Jordyn declared. She reached out to pat Willow's cheek.

"Thank you, sweetheart. Grandma says she wants to babysit you today. Is that all right?"

Jordyn shrugged exuberantly in one of those lovable gestures that made her look much older than three. "Okay."

As Willow double-checked that her cards and phone were secure in her lemon-printed wristlet, she half hoped Jordyn would start to fuss and ask her to stay, but her daughter was used to spending time with her family.

So what if Willow went on a trail ride with Ace? That didn't mean that today had to be the day she revealed the truth. It was her birthday, after all. Couldn't she pick another day to change everything and make him hate her forever?

Willow kissed the top of Jordyn's blond pigtails and hurried out of the diner before Aria could give her any more styling advice.

She blasted the Ladies of Country station on the way to Sommerton, so she could belt along with the radio instead of overthinking this whole endeavor. As was her custom for the last few years, she changed the station when she heard any ballads that sounded overly sad or sentimental.

By the time she pulled into Ernest Ranch's dirt lot, she was ready to kick the door open and conquer anything. But Ace was there waiting for her, and my, did he look handsome.

He wore his old Hoffmann Haven senior t-shirt, snug over his broad chest, and the forest green color made the verdant flecks in his hazel eyes shine like a kaleidoscope.

"You came," he said, as she stepped out of the car and slammed the door closed.

"I heard there was a cancellation fee," she grumbled.

Ace shook his head. "That's all Will's legal mumbo jumbo. I never enforce it."

Willow smiled. "Maybe that's why you're going broke."

Ace gestured toward the stables, and they strolled side by side. "We made a pretty penny at the Easter event." He sighed. "I'm sorry if I upset you the other day. You know I complain like an old mule. It's nothing personal."

A nervous laugh escaped Willow's lips. "Oh, my crying was nothing personal, either. Please don't worry about it. I get overwhelmed sometimes." That much was true.

Concern furrowed Ace's brow. He was such a nice person. And she... She had to stop thinking so much, or she would cry again.

They came up to the first building of horses, and she saw Arrow, Jack, and Sammy, just as she remembered them. She gravitated towards Sammy and stroked his brown and white forehead. He whinnied in recognition and leaned in close, almost like he was giving Willow a hug.

"Do you remember me, buddy?"

"I would say he does."

"Can I ride him?" She turned hopeful eyes on Ace.

"You would pick the most stubborn horse on the ranch."

Willow lifted her chin. "I'm more experienced than I was on our last trail ride. I remember what you told me about leading him straight."

"I think Arrow would make for an easier ride, but if you insist. You're the birthday girl."

Ace started tacking up his preferred horse, Jack. "You remember what to do?"

"I think so." She creaked open the wooden door to Sammy's stall and secured the latch behind her. She lifted his saddle pad and then swung the heavy saddle over his back, warning Sammy before each step in the process of what was about to happen. He shifted a bit and flicked his tail back and forth in annoyance.

She carefully roped his girth below his belly, and felt Ace's rough hands take over to tie it to the latigo. Of course he was already done saddling Jack. She stepped a safe distance away, so she wouldn't accidentally touch his hand again.

"Nicely done," he said. He quickly secured the knot, put on Sammy's bridle, and handed Willow the reins.

Ace used to lift Willow onto her horse, but this time, she led Sammy to the mounting block to place her left boot in the stirrup and swing her right leg over, settling in. Did Ace look disappointed, or was that Willow's imagination?

"Lead the way," she said.

Ace guided her onto a well-worn trail through the sunlit forest. Spring rains had made the green leaves of the sycamores come alive. There were even a few dogwoods in bloom, shedding their light, sweet fragrance in the air.

Willow felt like singing the opening notes to her dad's favorite musical until Sammy headed right for a tree, and a springy branch hit her in the face. "Hey, why are you going that way?"

She tugged the reins back to the left, but Sammy went too much to the left and departed from the trail again.

Ace expertly rode Jack back her way and tied Sammy's reins to his saddle horn.

She sighed, feeling like an amateur. "I know, you told me this was going to happen."

"I didn't say anything." But Ace was grinning.

"You didn't have to."

Riding the horses in tandem meant Ace and Willow were closer together. Their jeans lightly brushed a few times. Memories descended of autumn bonfires, evenings by the creek lit by fireflies. Movie nights with Ace and her family. Willow took time to study the clouds and suddenly wished the wood was not so quiet and tranquil. "Do people come for trail rides often?"

"Sure, especially on the weekend. Makes for a fun date." Ace cleared his throat and fell silent.

"I'm glad the rides are doing well."

"Thank you for how supportive you've been, helping us raise money."

Willow stroked the leather reins with her manicured nails. Now that Ace was leading, there was hardly anything for her to do. "You've built something beautiful here. It needs to keep going."

Ace's ears turned red, and Willow shook her head. He never could take a compliment.

Spending this much time together had knocked some honesty loose in Willow's chest. "I know I haven't always been supportive. The truth is, I felt a little jealous of how into the ranch you were."

It was understandable, considering how much Wyatt Ernest had given to Ace. How much Ace had always wanted to build something of his own. But having understandable motives hadn't made Ace's choice to cast her aside hurt any less.

"You were always the most important thing to me," Ace said, sending a shiver down Willow's back. "I'm sorry if I didn't make that clearer."

It felt good to have some closure. Closure was something Willow should have sought from the start, instead of running away from their problems, but even now, as a grown woman, when she tried to form the words to say, "Jordyn is your daughter. I'm so sorry I kept this from you. I was wrong," she simply couldn't.

Ace deserved to know—the squirming that grew in her heart told her that—but they were just starting to make progress. He had just started looking at her with appreciation instead mistrust. Willow never wanted it to end.

"We're coming back to the ranch." Ace looked down at his calloused hands. "I made you some pasta for lunch, if you're hungry. I wanted to make sure you got your favorite food. Not a heart attack served for breakfast because you're too nice to say no."

He remembered Dad's sugary morning tradition. "It's true, I never feel like I had to fluff you up to spare your feelings."

Ace brushed imaginary dust off of his bicep. "It's that tough skin of mine."

"But your pasta does come out nice, even on that tiny hot plate."

Ace puffed out his chest. Being a skilled cook must have been easier credit to accept than achieving his life's dream. "It should still be warm. I bought sweet tea and a baguette from the grocery store, too."

"Look at you, planning out a well-balanced meal."

Sammy whined nervously, and Jack took a few steps backward on the trail. Ace leaned forward. "What's wrong buddy? Come on, we're almost back home."

They emerged from the trees to the suffocating sensation of smoke. Willow's muscles stiffened. The building which housed Arrow, Jack, and Sammy's stalls was engulfed in hot flames.

Ace leapt off his mount, lifted Willow off of Sammy, and turned both horses loose. He could always find them later, but he didn't want to risk tying them to trees in case he couldn't get the fire under control.

He tossed Willow his phone. "Call 911, then the vet. His number's saved," he hollered.

"On it."

His plugged-in hot plate was far away from here, in the office building. So, what had happened?

Sammy's stall was burned away completely. The fire had turned to scarfing down the well-worn wood of Jack's. The normally tranquil

Arrow beat at her door with her hooves. Ace released her, sprinting out of her path as she burst out of her stall and into the woods. At least the horses were safe. Now, maybe they could minimize the damage.

Ace lined up all the ranch's feed buckets in a row in front of a spigot and let the water loose. When the first bucket was three-quarters full, Willow, who had snuck up behind Ace after her phone calls, said, "I'll fill the rest." This freed Ace up to dump the first bucket on the mighty inferno. The fire barely hissed in reply.

The bucketfuls wouldn't do much, but they'd keep on trying until the fire truck came. Raggedly, the pair repeated the cycle of fill, haul, dump, until the blessed sound of sirens screamed through the air, and the professionals took over, directing Ace and Willow to step back.

Ace winced as the force of the pressurized water slammed onto, yes, the fire, but also the remaining structure of the stables. The last half of boards fell limp onto the smoldering ashes.

Ace turned to Willow, her hair spilling out of her ponytail, sweat and dirt marring her arms, and pulled her in for a hug. He felt her shoulders begin to shake and allowed himself to stop moving and take in the gravity of what had just happened. What an incomprehensible nightmare. How could he afford to replace what he lost?

Willow stepped away and sniffed. "Do we need to get the horses now?"

Sweet Willow. As everything fell apart, here she was, constant, putting the force of her being behind making things all right again. He'd missed that.

"We'll worry about rounding them up in a few minutes. I'm going to talk to the firemen. Why don't you sit down in my office and get something to eat? The horses will be all right until then."

She nodded and headed towards the small outbuilding. Ace hoped sitting in a quiet place would help her calm down. He'd join her in a minute. First, he wanted to get some answers.

Ace recognized a man who he'd gone to high school with, Colby. He'd heard that Colby had achieved his dream of becoming a teacher, just like Willow. Sommerton was too small to have its own fire crew, so they relied on trained volunteers like Colby to pitch in after hours.

Ace reached out a hand to clasp Colby's thick protective glove. "Thanks, man. This could have been a lot worse if you guys hadn't gotten here so quickly."

"I'm just sorry it happened in the first place. We didn't find any reason why. No overturned lantern, no wiring on the building. I hate to ask this, but is there anyone who may have wanted to damage your property?"

Ace clamped his lips together. "Dan Achan's been trying to get me to sell for years now. Maybe he hoped I'd be so discouraged by a financial loss that I'd give it all up."

Colby spoke to another fireman, who had just finished winding up the waterlogged hose. "Jeff. Give the sheriff's office a call and have them find out where Dan Achan is." Colby looked toward Ace's office. "I'd better go make sure that Willow's all right."

A long-dormant protective instinct seized Ace's chest, and he put a hand out. "I was just going back there to check on her."

Colby raised his eyebrows. "Oh. All right. We'll finish up here. Let us know if you need any help rebuilding, man. We'll make a day of it."

"I appreciate that." It was good of Colby to offer up a piece of community well-doing, seeing as Ace had isolated himself from all others since graduation. He bought supplies, tended to the ranch's visitors and students, and that was about it.

Even a good old-fashioned barn raisin' wouldn't help Ace much now, not unless they donated every nail and scrap of lumber. All of Willow's changes had barely allowed him to break even this month. And now, they were back to square one.

The vet arrived then. Ace supposed Dr. Howell couldn't work pro bono again, but he had to make sure Arrow and the others hadn't suffered any damage, ingesting all that smoke. He hoped Willow was enjoying her meal, even if she had to be alone for another minute.

The doctor was good enough to help Ace retrieve the three horses from the woods. They hadn't roamed too far from home. Ace put Sammy in the open stall in the other set of stables, consoling him with a bucketful of cut carrots, and escorted the two gentler animals to the paddock. They would shelter there until replacement stables could be built.

"Arrow will be okay," the vet said, "but she needs to take it easy for a few weeks. Don't even tack her up for a trail ride." He'd have to use Jack for rides, then, to make sure Arrow healed completely. Just as soon as he got this mess cleaned up.

Next, the sheriff's deputy approached. Ace didn't know the man personally but recognized him from Sommerton's election posters.

"Mr. Sterling?" the deputy asked.

"That's me."

The vet excused himself with an apologetic smile. Ace sure liked the man but found it hard to return the smile when he knew he'd soon get another $500 bill in the mail that he was unable to pay.

The deputy cleared his throat. "I came to tell you that Dan Achan denies any wrongdoing. His father testified that he's been visiting at his house all day. There isn't currently any evidence to tie him to what happened."

"I understand. Thanks for looking into it for me."

"We'll let you know if we hear anything further."

Ace would ask Willow to have her dad pay a visit to Oliver Achan. The older man was a regular patron of Golden Days Diner, but would hardly be eager to incriminate his own son.

Dan very well may have been innocent, but this news was disappointing. Now Ace had no proof, no leads, and no one to help him pay for damages. Just a freak accident that may have just cost him his dream.

The last stranger at last cleared Ace's property. He ran to the office and was greeted with the aroma of sautéed red pepper and butter. Willow was talking on her cell, but said her goodbyes once she saw him come in.

"I was talking to my mom about what happened. She feels horrible. We all do."

His nerves settled down at the compassion in her eyes. In this moment, he wasn't facing his problems alone. Ace sat on a brown folding chair and spooned some noodles onto a paper plate. "This will put us back a bit more financially."

Willow chewed her lower lip. "How much is a bit?"

"Fifty-five hundred dollars."

She half-gasped, swiftly dousing her horror with a splash of cool confidence. "We'll have to plan another event, then."

"It won't be enough." Ace dropped his plastic spoon and ran his fingers through his tangled-up curls. Was this truly the end? He'd kept so busy trying to save the ranch, he hadn't really considered what he'd do if he couldn't. Failure had never been an option.

Closing down would devastate the community members who had made memories there for years. It would disprove Wyatt's faith in entrusting this place to him, leaving Ace nothing but an empty life and a stack of bills to pay. No, this couldn't be the end.

Willow's chirpy reply cut through his escalating terror. "The event will have to be bigger than the last one, of course."

"You've been watching too many of your dad's old movies. I have until the end of May before I'm reported to collections. My extensions have all passed."

Willow continued as if he hadn't spoken. "We're going to host a big dance in the barn. With line dancing! We'll bring in an instructor. Use some dollar store decorations. You can really elevate the most unexpected items with a little imagination. Don't you worry, I ignored your advice, and I saved everything we bought from the Easter tea." Sometimes Willow reminded Ace of a fairy-tale character. Like Snow White. Making something out of nothing.

"And how much will people be willing to pay for this?" She had surprised him with the number of guests that had come to their last event.

"Oh, thirty dollars at least. For a night on the town, in a real country barn? I'll hold auditions at the school for a solo musician. The kids will love that, and it's free publicity to draw their parents in. We'll get donations from local businesses and hold a silent auction."

"I don't have connections with any local businesses."

Willow tsked. "My parents are Hoffmann Haven Chamber of Commerce members, remember?"

Ace had a hard time resurrecting the hope from his heart that had plummeted to the ground the moment he'd felt the heat of the fire, as he watched the forward motion they'd made reverse tenfold. But he infused energy back into his tone, for Willow's sake. "Is there anything that I have to do, Miss President?"

"Believe me, I'll let you know." Her eyes sparkled with mischief. A couple of gentle creases had formed beside them in the last few years, but the marks in no way diminished her beauty. On the contrary, Ace thrilled that he'd been given the opportunity to see Willow grow and change again, and that she'd still found reasons to laugh and smile during their separation.

Maybe Willow had made a deeply hurtful and impulsive choice to end their relationship based on the things that he'd said. Things that he'd said, feared, meant, but now realized he'd secretly hoped that Willow would convince him weren't true. After all, wasn't a potential life partner supposed to believe in you more than anyone? More than even yourself?

Ace wasn't sure what had happened between the two of them, but perhaps he'd been wrong too, in letting Willow go so easily. Cutting people out of his life after they rejected him was a coping mechanism that had saved his life in childhood, after his birth parents' downward spiral, but it might have also cost him the most important person in his life.

He wouldn't force any romantic feelings on her if her love was already gone, but one thing Ace felt sure of. If she showed any more signs of wanting to rekindle their relationship, he was in.

6

It had been a week since Willow had announced to her fifth period chorale class that they would hold a competition to see which musical act would perform at the barn dance benefit for Ernest Ranch.

Rehearsals had been in full force since then. Bo Ernest usually faded to the back of the bass section but seemed to really want the chance to support his grandfather's ranch. He had even asked to bring in his guitar.

Hoffmann Haven High had blessed the choir program with three wide levels of raised, cream-colored flooring, so they didn't have to worry about teenagers fitting on the narrow standalone ones that other schools were stuck with.

The typical vocal divisions had flown out the window. Sopranos planned duets with altos. One tenor moved his chair in the back corner of the room so that no one could overhear the song he chose until the official tryout.

Aria would sing a country duet with her friend Samantha. Their tone was sweet and pure, but Willow couldn't show any favoritism. The front runner would be determined today.

Act after act came forward. Some displayed a characteristic last-minute effort. Others went above and beyond with their stage presence, coordinating outfits and striking a few dance moves.

Bo was the last contestant. He chose to perform seated. He cleared his throat, and his rich, low vibrato reached out to captivate the entire room.

Lady, I love you,
    But you're just out of my reach.
    Guess I can't have you,
    'Cause I'm too afraid to speak.

Been dreamin' about you
    Throughout the lonely years.
    If only our distance
    Could be closed up with my tears.

Bo's eyes met Aria's on the last note, and he blushed furiously. "Miss Hutchins, that's all I had time for. I'm having trouble coming up with a third verse."

"You wrote that?" Willow had thought Bo had drawn from some obscure Conway or Hank record. "You're so talented, Bo."

He stared down at his guitar. "Thanks, ma'am."

Willow thought she would need more time to review her notes before declaring the winner, but she announced, "I think Bo's original song is perfect to sing at the benefit."

The kids all clapped and hollered.

Bo looked up. "Really?"

Willow nodded. "Absolutely. I'll help you finish the song. Think you could come here during your lunch tomorrow?"

"Sure thing."

The afternoon flew by, her beginner-level choir classes abuzz with stories about Bo's song last hour. Then it was the home shift, managing dinner, bath, and bedtime for Jordyn. After she straightened Jordyn's dolls in their cozy living room and did the dishes, Willow crashed into her bed, only for her alarm to wake her far too soon.

Coffee and leftover egg casserole from the diner fueled her through kissing her sweet, sleepy girl goodbye, dropping her off with Grandma, making the short drive to work, and preparing her classroom for her morning music history classes.

Despite the early hour, her music history kiddos were always rowdy, since they were there for the fine arts credit instead of by choice. But she did her best to share her love of the different genres and forms of expression, and to make the students feel welcomed above all.

During fourth period lunch, Aria knocked on Willow's classroom door, but Willow handed her lunch bag and shooed her away, not sure if Bo would want an audience for the composition process.

Soon after, Bo arrived with a sack lunch in hand. He put his backpack down by his guitar, and Willow insisted that he join her to eat before they dove in to writing.

"How was third period?" she asked him.

"It's math," he intoned, as if the word alone was enough explanation.

"Sorry. How's Ace holding up?" Images of his face had haunted her since the fire. He'd done his best to appear strong, but carefree, joking Ace had been washed away by the force of his loss, leaving only despondency and defeat.

"He's down about the fire damage, no doubt about that, but he started rebuilding the stables."

"How?"

"On more credit." He grimaced.

"I feel like we just made progress and for this to happen..." Willow slammed down her turkey wrap. "Well, we'll just have to do our best with the rest of this song!"

"I'm glad I can help in some way. I just hope it's enough."

Willow placed a gentle hand on his shoulder. It was a lot of pressure for a young man to put on himself. "Me, too. But I'm sure Ace will be proud of you, no matter what. Did you tell him yet that you were chosen to sing?"

"Yeah, and I told him we were finishing up the song together. When is the benefit?"

"Two weeks from now, on May second. We decided that date would strike a good balance between giving us time to advertise and getting the ranch the money it needs. Aria's picking up copies of our promo flyer from the library later today—the principal agreed to let us post them around the school."

"Can you give me some copies in class tomorrow? I'll take them all around town."

"Sure thing." Everyone who'd heard about the fire had been eager to help, but Willow was sure the news had been the hardest on Bo, who grew up on his grandpa's ranch.

She hoped having tasks to complete would provide him some distraction before the big night.

Bo devoured his sandwich, chips, apple, and cookie in short order, plus the chocolate milk that surely was wreaking havoc on his vocal cords. It was fine, though. Right now, they needed to concentrate on the quality of the lyrics, not the sound.

"Should we get started?" Willow asked, and Bo nodded, picking up his guitar.

She stepped out from her desk to join him at his usual spot in the highest level of the room's center, pulling out a student chair to sit on while they worked. Bo produced what he'd written so far in a spiral notebook for Willow to purview with her purple ink pen.

"What we need to figure out is where this song is going. You've been longing and sorrowful. Will you give your listeners a happy ending, or leave it open-ended?"

Bo considered for a moment. "I think I'd like a happy ending."

"And what would that look like? What would it feel like?"

"Like relief after a horrible storm. Like I'd gone through all the waiting, all the fear, and it was worth it."

"That's great!" Willow reached for the guitar and Bo handed it over. She wasn't a skillful player but recalled the few simple chords that made up Bo's melody and started strumming.

We found our way together,
  Though the floods were rising high,
I'll love you forever.
I'll love you 'till I die.

She laughed, a little self-conscious. "That's probably overly romantic. But, did anything feel authentic to what you were trying to say?"

"No, miss, that's perfect! You sure sound like you know what you're talking about."

Now Willow was the one blushing. She hoped he wasn't

entertaining any ideas about her and Ace getting back together. She'd sensed last week that he was beginning to open up again, but would she? The problems of their past felt too large to overcome. Willow still couldn't see how their story could have a happy ending, no matter how much she might wish for it.

Ace hung burlap bows from the tops of the barn walls as Bo and Willow fiddled with the sound system up front. Why the bows had to be way up here, only reachable by ladder, to look good, Ace didn't know, but this was all Willow's show now, and he would happily play the stagehand if all these shenanigans pulled together to make a miracle.

Willow had borrowed the small amp from an old classmate for free for the week and made sure the mic was working for Bo's song. Bo had agreed to learn a slew of country classics plus modern hits to sing that would work well as line dances, so there was no need to hire a D.J., which was great news for their meager budget.

Ace descended to adjust the ladder once again, leaving the box with the bows and string lights on the top rung. He heard Willow say, "Why don't you run through your song, Bo? Make sure you feel comfortable before next Saturday." Ace scooted the ladder to the left but then leaned on it and turned towards the makeshift stage he'd built. Bo had been downright secretive about his song since he'd told Ace he would be singing for the fundraiser, and Ace had been curious to hear what he and Willow had come up with.

Bo did a quick tune-up before starting to strum. His posture straightened impressively as he took on the persona of a stage star. That was likely due to Willow's coaching.

Bo looked out across the crowd, though his only listeners were Ace and Willow. "Hi there, folks, thanks for coming out. I'd like to share a little something that I wrote with the help of my music teacher. Hope y'all like it."

He closed his eyes and crooned,

Lady, I love you,
> *But you're just out of my reach.*
> *Guess I can't have you,*

'Cause I'm too afraid to speak.

Been dreamin' about you
Throughout the lonely years.
If only our distance
Could be closed up with my tears.

His voice was all heartbreak until he picked up the tempo to a jaunty finish, even stomping his boot and leaning over the mic.

We found our way together,
Though the floods were rising high,
I'll love you forever.
I'll love you 'till I die.

He held the last note and said, "Real love endures. Hope y'all take that message back home with ya."

Ace burst into applause. "Who's this big shot, and what have you done with little Bo Ernest?"

"Was it okay?"

"Okay? Once word spreads of us hosting a concert for a future bona-fide country star, we'll be turning people away at the door."

"Aw, Ace, don't go on about me. I wouldn't do this at all, except I love the ranch so much."

"That means a lot, brother. Thanks for stepping in the spotlight for us."

Willow added, "And if everyone gets to see how talented you are, so much the better." Bo took the praise more graciously from the lady, but still, his eyes dropped down to his shoes.

She turned to Ace. "How did the sound system work from over there?"

"Clear as a whistle. I heard a bit of an echo, but once we finish decorating, that shouldn't be a problem."

"We can afford to crank the volume up a bit if needed. I'll bring Aria with us next week. She'll help make sure everything runs smooth."

Ace returned to hanging bows. "Patrick and Riley aren't coming?"

"On a Saturday?" Willow sounded bemused. "Dad's not hosting music night so they won't draw our whole crowd away. But they make too much money on the weekends to close up the diner, even though they want to."

Bo packed his guitar into his case. "Ya'll need any help?"

"Nah. We've got it handled, right, Willow?"

"We're almost done, I promise. Have a good night, Bo."

"Good night, miss."

His boots stomped over the stage, he hopped off, and soon the barn door slammed shut, leaving only the two of them. Ace hung the bows even faster. Willow stepped beside him and picked up the wad of lights to feed him a bit of string at a time so he wouldn't waste time reaching down and untangling.

Ace looked back toward the closed door. "That kid spends too much time around here. I don't ever see him hanging out with friends."

Willow said, "Hmm. Sounds like somebody else I know."

"Yeah, yeah. He's doing all right in school, though?"

"Bo's a great student. Keeps to himself, but there's nothing wrong with that."

"From that song he wrote, it sounds like he has a crush."

"Most likely."

Ace didn't want to rat Bo out and tell Willow he suspected it was Aria. "You all did a nice job with the lyrics." He turned to look into her cobalt-blue eyes. "How much did you have to help him?"

Her cheeks pinked. "He wrote it all, except for the last verse."

He pressed farther. "You mean the part that went, 'I'll love you 'till I die?'"

"Mm-hmm." She examined the lights, as if she was going to check every bulb, but the tension between them was as inescapable as waves along the shore. If only she would admit her feelings, instead of hiding from them.

He stepped off the ladder. That got her attention.

"Wha-what are you doing?" she asked, putting the lights down to run her fingers through the ends of her hair.

"Seeing if you want to kiss me as much as I want to kiss you." What kind of a fool thing was that to say? He never was good at keeping his fast-talking thoughts to himself. It was just that, their first kiss had been in this barn. Did she remember?

Willow buried her face in her hands. Ace thought he'd embarrassed her, until she started to cry.

"Good grief, Willow, I'm sorry. I won't bring up kissing again."

"It's not that. I do want to kiss you. That's what makes this so horrible."

Ace's heart leapt and he peeled Willow's hands from off her wet eyes. "Makes what so horrible?"

"You don't know everything about me."

He gripped her hands. "Of course I do. I've known you since we were fourteen. You're the most gorgeous, talented, special girl alive, and your only weakness is falling for a blockhead like me."

That just made her cry harder.

"Really, now, Willow. What's wrong?"

Willow plucked her hands away to wipe her eyes, and a cold breeze blew over his palms from their absence. She stood straighter and said, "Jordyn is your daughter."

"What?" Ace felt his body freeze from his heart up to his brain and clear down to his toes. Somehow, he thawed out his mouth. "Jordyn is my..."

"There never was a rebound guy. He was just a cover, so you'd leave us be."

"You wanted me to leave you be?"

"No, I didn't want you to feel obligated to stay just because we spent the night together before we should have. I wanted you to *want* to start a family with me."

His mind spun, trying to decode her words and see her perspective. "You thought I couldn't want to start a family with you, so you decided not to give me a chance at all?"

Willow spoke quickly. "If I could do it over, I would. But the thought of forcing you to marry me, to give up the ranch was unbearable. I thought this way I could make sure Jordyn never felt rejected."

"Because you felt rejected by my work out here."

"Well, yes."

He said the next words without emotion. "Then, I'm just a bruised up foster kid who can't commit to anyone living, is that right?"

Willow clenched her fists defensively. "You're the one who said you couldn't be a father, not me." Was she blaming this on him?

Her voice grew mournful. "I just wanted to be something that you wanted more than anything. I'm sorry I let my feelings bleed over to what may have been best for you and Jordyn."

Him and Jordyn. Father and daughter. He'd missed three years of her life, not to mention the time when she was a tiny baby in Willow's womb.

"Ace, please say something." Her eyes pleaded for his mercy, his forgiveness.

Ace shook his head. He used to indulge Willow with little things she wanted back when she was his girl, but now she was asking for what he didn't have to give. Clarity, balance, wisdom. Anything but the raw hurt he was feeling.

"I know we were both young. But you could have given me a say in what happened in our relationship, and with my own kid. I don't know what feels worse. The moments I'll never get back, or your lack of faith in me. I mean, what did you think I was going to do? Run out of town? Become my parents?"

Willow's tears ran thicker from his condemnation, but she repeated, "I didn't know if you would run away, or if you would stay and not really love us. Either option was awful."

"What about the option where I would have loved and been good to you both." Ace shoved the ladder against the wall, and the bow he'd just hung came swinging off the nail. Sort of like the life Ace had built, now torpedoing out of control. "I'm sorry, Willow, I can't do this right now."

He stormed off and got in his truck. He needed more time to process, to think through what he was going to do with the information he'd just learned. Willow's doubts hung heavy on one of his shoulders and his regrets on the other.

7

After Ace had returned from his hours-long drive last night to check on the horses, he'd noticed that Willow had finished decorating by herself. A silent apology maybe, but one he still couldn't receive.

Now, he was finishing up his hot day at the Sommerton Train Station. He'd changed the oil, checked the wheels, and recorded the maintenance he'd done on the passenger train which had swept through town this morning. With his paperwork filed, Ace was free to pull off his filthy orange safety vest and stand by the Missouri river.

The water was tranquil, smooth, and still, but it did nothing to calm his insides. He'd been so desperate by his lunch hour that he'd texted Will Ernest, who'd agreed to meet Ace waterside after finishing his own work for the day.

The two of them used to hang out here all the time, back when Will's father Wyatt was still alive, Will hadn't yet opened his own law practice, and Ace didn't have so much to do on the ranch. But tension had burrowed in their relationship like chickweed, and Ace wondered if it was, in part, because sober-minded Will resented how thrilled Wyatt was to have found another crazy dreamer who loved the horses as much as he did.

Ace'd felt honored, but a little guilty, that he'd been included in the Ernest inheritance alongside Wyatt's natural-born son. Yet, the Bible taught that he was adopted, important, and loved, no matter what his worldly status was. He was determined not to sink in the mire of his past, but instead, to do his best with the chance he'd been given.

One thing Ace knew. Mr. Ernest wouldn't like to see "his boys" with so much separation between them now. It was a good sign for their friendship that Will had made the time for Ace, when it counted the most. Ace had to talk to someone about the bombshell Willow dropped, or he'd explode.

Will's well-waxed sports car pulled into the small lot beside the river.

Ace hardly waited for the door to slam shut before saying, "I just found out I'm a father." The words sounded completely foreign to his ears.

The typically self-possessed attorney's jaw shot open. "To Willow's girl?"

Ace nodded. In retrospect, he didn't know how he'd believed Willow would run off and have a fling so easily when everyone knew she had been devoted to Ace. He guessed that it had just been simpler to cut her out of his heart than risk thinking too deeply about what happened.

"And how are you feeling?"

Will's preference toward asking good questions over launching into unsolicited advice was another quality that made him a top-notch lawyer.

"Mixed-up. Terrified." Ace pushed the dirt beneath his steel-toed boots as if it were the same dirt, the same world that existed yesterday. "I guess she didn't trust me to be a family man."

Will unbuttoned and rolled up his shirtsleeves. "That's ridiculous. You're the most determined man I know."

"Determined to do what, though? She thinks I should have been more focused on her, and she took some things I said to heart that maybe I shouldn't have said."

"I think most people are guilty of saying things they don't mean. She still should have told you."

Ace's shoulders drooped. "She was sorry. She knew I had the right to know."

"Well, that's a start. I'm sure it was hard for her, to find out she was pregnant after graduation."

"I would have helped her." Ace's eyes bored into Will's and found great relief in the confidence staring back at him.

"I know you would have." Will wiped a bead of sweat from his brow. He was still in his wool dress pants, shirt, and suit vest, bless him. "So, what's next?"

"Part of me felt like starting up in a new town again. Leaving what she did to me behind and letting her live with the consequences. Of course, then I'd be proving her right, that I'm spineless and unfit to be called a father."

"I'm glad you waited to talk more until you could cool down a bit, but the two of you are going to have to work this out, soon. I have a lot of experience negotiating custody, visitation rights, child support..."

"Whoa," Ace cut Will off. "Your advice is welcome, but I'm not thinking contracts and law offices yet. Willow is all this little girl knows. I'm not going to try and take her away for half the time. I'm hoping Willow is willing to let me spend some time with Jordyn," a tight rubber band snapped over Ace's heart at the thought of getting the little girl to like him, "and I'm going to let her know that I plan to help from now on."

"The fact that Willow came to you is a good sign," Will agreed. "You let me know if you need anything."

"Thanks, man. Just knowing you're there for me helps a lot. Now, get home to Bo."

Will grinned. "He's already ordered takeout."

"Wouldn't want it to get cold."

Ace watched Will drive away and wondered if he'd ever have a family to get home to. Then, he took a deep breath, and texted Willow.

Profound relief had replaced the nagging anxiety which had marked every moment until Ace reached out. Willow'd thought about calling, sending messages to reiterate just how sorry she was, but she knew he had to take the next step. He'd suggested that they meet Tuesday night at Suzy's Dessert Bar, which coincidentally had been the spot of their first date.

Inside, the walls were bright purple, and a wall of swirling soft serve in every flavor ended with a buffet of brownies, candy pieces, mashed fresh cookies, and even frosting. A truly irresistible outing.

Jordyn loved coming here, but Willow left her with Riley so she could fully concentrate on what Ace had to say. Maybe they'd all come here together one day, but that seemed too much to hope for.

She hadn't told her mother what had transpired the night before. She just said that she needed a few hours alone. Willow was anticipating that she'd have more positive news after the meeting. She'd rather not report the current state of affairs: "Ace looked like I punched him in the gut and then ran off!"

Willow meandered through the dessert bar, collecting banana ice cream, whipped cream, maraschino cherries, and chocolate chips. This heart attack on a plate wasn't going to do her nerves any favors, but at least she'd have somewhere else to look besides Ace's wounded expression this time.

Ace came in and nodded to Willow and Suzy, whose hand froze over the cash register mid-tap. But the business owner finished Willow's transaction, thankfully less nosy than some other townspeople may have been.

Ace loaded up his plate with all the candy he wanted like a big kid with awesome metabolism, and Willow had to smile, despite the tense occasion. He joined her at a small table, away from the front windows.

"Thanks for meeting with me," Willow said softly.

"Sure. I figured we should talk about what the future might look like."

Willow stirred her whipped cream nervously, but Ace said, "I say we take things slow and steady, one day at a time. This will be a big adjustment for everyone."

She dropped her spoon. "She's my whole world, Ace. And I know I should have let you be a part of hers sooner, but I'm scared she'll get upset." Willow drew in a deep breath. She hadn't intended to communicate more uncertainty. It was just so hard to imagine how they all were going to interact with each other.

Ace fixed his hazel eyes on her. "I know I'm not going to be a perfect father. Lord knows I had a bad enough example."

"You had a wonderful one, too, in Wyatt Ernest. I should have focused more on that, instead of on the negative all the time."

"First off, I'd like to help out financially."

"I don't expect you to—"

He put his hand up to halt her objections. "I'll prioritize family. If I can't afford to do that, then I haven't a right to keep the ranch going."

"At least wait until after the benefit. Then maybe you can help with a few things, like when I get her some bigger clothes soon. Really, we've been doing okay, though. God's blessed us with everything we need, and Mom and Dad are a big help."

"I know you've been doing fine without me." Ace didn't sound as mad as he did last night. More solemn and disappointed.

"That's not what I'm trying to say. I know that the older Jordyn gets, the more she will need her father. Maybe we can go on an outing together, so she gets to know you and feel more comfortable."

"I'd like that."

"We can tell her the news together, so she can see you and hopefully start to understand."

"That sounds good. Is there any time this week that would work?"

Willow pulled up the calendar on her phone. "Well, we have ballet class Thursday at six."

"At that little studio downtown?"

"Yes." Suzy had really cranked up the A.C. in there, and a shiver ran over Willow's arms at the thought of this monumental meetup happening in front of all the dance moms in town. However, she was thankful that Ace did seem to want to be involved, and she didn't want to bar him any more with her worries.

"All right. I'll see you there, then. The parents gather by the glass outside the practice room and can watch the whole lesson. The kids are pretty adorable at this age."

Ace swallowed, looking slightly daunted as well. But he simply said, "I bet they are."

Then, they talked details about Saturday's fundraiser until both of their treats were gone and they parted ways until Thursday. Willow would be on pins and needles until then.

It was surreal, driving to downtown Hoffmann Haven for the second time this week, when previously, Ace hadn't been there for years. The evening sky had darkened overhead, bringing a chill to the air.

The dance studio was a familiar fixture not too far from Suzy's Dessert Bar, its windows covered by paint pen drawings of cheerful blue Easter baskets stuffed with eggs, and a bunny with a leotard and pointe shoes on.

As he parallel-parked, he caught a glimpse of Willow and Jordyn through his rearview window, sporting matching lavender jackets, seated on a wrought-iron park bench. Ace's stomach spun like the steering wheel of his truck.

He grabbed the handful of bluebells he'd picked from the edge of the woods earlier, hoping the gesture wouldn't seem too much for the occasion. He approached the girls, and Willow invited him to sit on her left side, while Jordyn side-eyed him from her right.

"Hey," she said. "I figured we'd better do this outside, just in case."

Ace nodded and handed Jordyn the bouquet. She wrapped her small hands around the bundle and held it tightly to her chest. "Pretty."

Willow rubbed Jordyn's back. "Jordyn. This is Ace. He's your daddy."

Jordyn regarded him over her armful of blooms. "Daddy?"

"That's right," Ace said.

"Naw." Jordyn grinned.

Willow pinched her lips together. "I'm not joking, sweetheart. It's true. Ace is your daddy. He's come to watch your ballet lesson today."

Jordyn leapt up and spun, her pink chiffon skirt twirling around her. "I'm a ballerina!"

Ace chuckled. "Yes, I can see that. You're very good."

This earned him a smile that melted his heart into a puddle, like a chocolate bar on a scorching day.

Jordyn tweaked her leg back and her arm forward in a ballerina pose so ferociously that he had to laugh. She was adorable. Willow's spitting image, attitude and all.

"Don't laugh at me." Jordyn crossed her arms and stuck out her bottom lip.

Ace schooled his expression. "I'm sorry. I wasn't laughing at you. I'm just happy because I liked your dance so much."

Mollified, Jordyn threw her arms in the air and continued dancing to the music in her mind.

"All right, all right, that's enough. Save some energy for your lesson." Willow led the way through the studio's reception room, down a narrow hallway, to a row of chairs for the parents. Willow removed Jordyn's jacket, and kissed the top of her braided head. "Have a great time, sweet pea."

"See you next week!" Jordyn flung her flowers into Ace's lap, waved proudly, and strode into the studio to greet her tiny friends with hugs.

"She's great, Willow. You've done an amazing job."

Willow fiddled with the fuchsia strap of Jordyn's dance bag. "Thanks. That's nice to hear, but not sure how much I had to do with it. She's been amazing me since the day she was born. Jordyn is heaven-sent."

Though Ace hadn't got to pitch in like he would have liked, he still felt a lightning bolt of pride when he saw Jordyn shine at the barre, following the teacher's instructions eagerly. That was his blond hair. His mama's hair, passed down to this perfect little angel.

"Ace Sterling?" A high-pitched voice interrupted his observation. "I haven't seen you around here in a while."

Ace turned to look more closely at the mom to his right and withheld a sigh. He hadn't recognized her at first, since her hair was piled on her head in a messy bun instead of perfectly straightened, but it was a girl—Raena?—from their graduating class.

"Hey there, good to see you," he said.

It took approximately two seconds for Raena to eye the flowers in Ace's hand and blurt out, "Are you two back together? I always felt so bad about what happened."

Ace and Willow had been voted "most likely to get married" in their senior class superlatives, by a landslide. Ace should have known better than to think they could sneak by the public and get reacquainted gradually, but he wasn't going to back down now. "I'm just here supporting a friend, but thank you."

Raena opened her mouth as if to say more, but Ace threw a quick glance at Willow, to make sure she hadn't been offended by his choice of words. Then, he faced straight ahead to watch the class through the glass.

After a few basic exercises which the tykes tried to replicate with varying levels of success, they were allowed to jump around and have fun as kids music played. He noticed that Jordyn was mouthing the words to several songs.

"Smart little thing, isn't she?" He turned to Willow, who was dabbing her eyes with a tissue, but she looked happy this time.

"Sharp as a tack. I'm glad I get to share this with you, Ace."

"I'm glad, too."

Maybe Willow had worried that Ace would dredge up the past and berate her again, but he was determined to accept his share of the blame for creating her doubts in the first place, put aside his pain as best he could, and move forward. If tonight was any indication, their future was looking pretty bright.

8

Willow's dress for the barn dance was a soft pink, Ace's favorite color on her. But that wasn't why she'd chosen it, was it?

The sleeves poofed out in a lovely, feminine way, but the sweetheart bodice was cut tight into a full skirt. Perfect for movement if she got out on the dance floor.

Her cowboy boots completed the ensemble, of course. They had been a one-year anniversary gift from Ace, a practical leather pair for ranch visiting, but stitched with a feather-like design in a funky shade of teal to appeal to Willow's sense of style.

Willow had secured her curled hair on the crown of her head in a bun with a crystal-studded ribbon. Though the hour was growing later, and Ace had promised to install fans around the barn, she wanted to be sure she felt as cool and collected as possible.

That was going to be a challenge, however, if her memory of Ace the other night served her right. The pure love and adoration that had shone from his eyes as he watched Jordyn dance had filled her with relief, and a little sadness that she had been so wrong about what kind of father he would make.

As awkward as Ace must have felt at such a significant meet-up, seeing as his only experience with little children was his job at the ranch, he had done phenomenally showering Jordyn with attention. Dancing had never been Ace's favorite, but he'd put that aside, because it was what Jordyn loved to do.

Willow was in danger of contemplating whether he'd overcome his aversion a second time tonight, when she'd be on the dance floor, until Jordyn burst through the door.

"Mommy? You're putting on your make-up?" She popped her lips with the last syllable.

"Yes, I am. Would you like to watch?"

"I put on your make-up."

"Uh..." Willow chuckled. She'd made that mistake before. "You can help me put on my blush." Something that would be easy to correct if Jordyn became over-zealous with the application.

Very seriously, Jordyn dipped the blush in the rose-colored powder and brushed it gently over Willow's cheeks.

"Thank you. Good job." Willow brushed on her favorite sheer eye shadow and applied dark mascara and shimmery gloss.

"You're sparkly!" Jordyn declared.

"I like to be sparkly." Willow laughed.

"I want to be sparkly, too."

"Let's see what we can find in your closet."

Jordyn was delighted to be staying up past her bedtime, and even more so if that meant dressing fancy.

"I want that one." She pointed to a white flower girl dress she'd worn to the wedding of one of Willow's friends. The gossamer material would surely get dirty, but tonight was a special occasion.

"All right. But you have to wear your white sneakers to match."

Jordyn said, "Okay," a welcome concession, since she usually insisted upon strappy sandals or Mary Janes.

Willow found Jordyn's lace-topped socks and swept her fair curls into pigtails. Jordyn skipped over to her teddy bear jewelry box and slid a clear bead necklace all the way up her arm. "Now I'm ready," she said.

"Great. Let's go pick up Auntie Aria."

Aria hopped in the passenger seat from the sidewalk in front of the diner. She lifted her eyebrows and said, "You look nice."

"So do you," Willow said, just as suggestively. Aria wore a yellow dress patterned with baby's breath—all country cuteness. She sported the diamond-studded golden hoops that Willow had bought her for Christmas, and she'd seemed to take extra time in painting on smoky eyes and dark lips.

Willow started the winding drive toward Sommerton.

"It's an important night for the ranch," Aria explained. "For the choir. And for the two of us, since we pitched in so much."

Willow purposefully relaxed her shoulders, which were in danger of seizing up to her ears with stress. "I know. I've been so busy preparing that my nerves are just now starting to kick in." She'd been busy preparing and dealing with a personal crisis.

She'd need to tell Aria about Ace being Jordyn's father soon after the dance. Willow had learned her lesson about keeping secrets.

"But we've done all we can, and now it's up to the community to show up. Let's try and have a nice time." Willow was glad Jordyn was with her. Enjoying her little girl's reactions would be a welcome distraction from feeling all the pressure of executing an event well done.

She parked her car next to Ace's truck. Bo's car was here already, too. Hand-chalked blackboards led them to the barn. Ace had blessedly scooped any animal leavings away, and the walk to the dance was surprisingly pleasant-smelling. In the air was only the scents of hay, tiki torches, and the pair of potted indigo bushes Willow'd bought to line the doorway.

They had arrived early, but not crazy early for Jordyn's sake. The green-skirted tables holding the raffle baskets, which would be under Aria's command, were already set up. Bo was hooking his guitar up to the sound system, and Ace was putting the finishing touches on their charcuterie station.

He'd successfully made the punch and arranged the cute paper cups Willow had ordered with Ernest Ranch's horses on the front to be ready for their guests. The refreshment table would be Willow's domain—a station that she could easily abandon if Jordyn got fussy. Plastic jugs of less fancy pink lemonade were stowed beneath the tablecloth, since the guests would likely be dancing up a storm and draining the punchbowl dry all night.

"Where's Lindsey?" Willow asked, looking back through the door for the energetic dance instructor. It would be a disaster if they hosted a line dance with no dancing.

"Dunno. I might have to call the moves out if she forgot." Ace shook his hips in a lame imitation of real choreography.

That was Ace, always joking around when Willow was on the verge of losing her head.

"I'm here," Lindsay called from the entrance, stunning in a black sequined bodysuit and denim skirt.

"Thank goodness. A professional." They hadn't known Lindsay when they found her information online, but she had given them a great rate once she discovered that the dance would be for charity. Another huge blessing in the planning process.

Lindsay joined Bo to go over the set list they'd collaborated on, and Ace joined Willow, Aria, and Jordyn at the barn's center. "Well, don't you three ladies look beautiful," he said.

Jordyn preened. "Hey, Daddy!"

Willow looked to Aria, panicked.

"That's cute," Aria said. "She thinks you're her daddy. You must have made a good impression the day of the Easter tea. I know she likes being out here."

"Aria." Willow gripped Ari's shoulder. She swallowed to wet her suddenly parched throat. "Ace is her daddy."

"What?" Aria blinked several times. Her eyes narrowed. "Why did you tell us it was that other guy?"

Willow shook her head. "I'm sorry. I thought we'd be safer pushing Ace away, but I only created the hurt I'd feared. Please forgive me."

Aria's gaze bounced between Willow and Ace. Then, she squeezed both of their hands. "Willow and Ace, back together again. This is great news!"

Willow's returning smile was a bit forced. She wondered what extent of "back together" Aria meant. Willow wasn't avoiding Ace, or the truth, anymore, but beyond that, she didn't know. Now she had to worry about Jordyn *and* Aria being disappointed if things didn't pan out between her and Ace. At least Aria wasn't holding a grudge about Willow's lie.

After that, Will Ernest strolled in. Willow was touched to see him here—usually he avoided the ranch like the plague.

"Our first guest." Ace threw his arms open wide.

Will grimaced. "The perks of owning my own law practice. I hope this doesn't mean I have to help set up."

Ace closed one arm around his friend. "Don't you worry about a thing. You're here to enjoy a wonderful evening. Aria, why don't you show Will our raffle baskets? There's a Sommerton Steakhouse one that's sure to catch your eye."

Will harrumphed but followed the teen. Aria settled into her role like a regular Vanna White, launching into the details of each selection.

Willow took Jordyn to sit behind the snack table. She was able to breathe once she saw the steady stream of people stopping by Ace's check-in station. The turnout was even better than they'd expected. Some were from Hoffmann Haven, some from Sommerton, and many she didn't recognize at all.

Ace greeted each and every one with an emphatic handshake, and, about twenty minutes in, Lindsay and Bo got three rows of dancers on the floor.

"Follow along with me," Lindsay yelled. "If you get lost, just jump right back in!"

The crowd's initial attempts were hard to watch, but they soon got used to repeated combinations of stomping, kicking, pivoting, and grapevining. Most of all, it was great to watch people young and old loosen up and laugh together. Eventually, their footfalls turned into a synchronized, energetic extension of Bo's music, of their shared community.

After a half-hour of constant dancing, Lindsay headed to the refreshment table for a break. "Hey, why don't you guys get out there and dance? I can cover the snacks."

"Thanks." Jordyn had been getting wiggly.

Hawk-eyed Aria saw them leaving their post and abandoned hers as well. "No one's coming by anymore. I sold hundreds of tickets, though!"

"That's fine. Enjoy yourself. Maybe Ace can make one more announcement before the night is through."

Aria ran over to some of Willow's choir kids, who waved to her and Jordyn. Willow waved back, thankful to have the opportunity to build a tight relationship with her students and their families outside of school. They'd been an amazing support for this effort.

"It's going well, I think." Ace's eager voice materialized behind Willow's left ear, and she shivered in spite of herself.

She fanned herself with her hand. "I'd say so."

"I owe all of this to you. I think we're going to do it." Ace was practically bouncing out of his boots. "Even if we don't, I'm glad we gave it one last try."

"It is a wonderful place, when we all come together like this. I'm sorry if I couldn't always see that."

"Don't apologize." Ace squeezed her hand and immediately let it go, though Willow wished he wouldn't have. He looked so handsome in his gray striped button-up.

Bo's next song was his soft ballad, and Willow was surprised to see Aria hop up on stage with him. Maybe to provide background vocals? But no, as Bo plucked the same two notes over and over again, Aria said, "Let's give it up for the amazing sponsors of today's event, Ace Sterling and Willow Hutchins!"

The barn echoed with shouts and whistles.

As Bo began to croon, his opening words husky and low, Aria hurried off the stage to Willow and Ace, scooping Jordyn up and swirling her around in a circle. "I meant, get dancing you two, if that wasn't clear."

There were a few couples out on the floor, but many of the guests were still watching Willow and Ace, standing there stiff as a pair of boards. Then, Ace extended his hand. "Do you want to?"

"I will," Willow answered, though what she meant was, *I want to very badly.*

She inhaled his woodsy aftershave and relished the feeling of his strong arms holding her close again. Maybe not as close as he used to, but she was content to take things slow, enjoy the moment, and hope for more moments just like this.

Willow had agreed to dance. Not only that, but she clasped Ace's hand as if pleading for him to never let her go again. After a few steps together, she relaxed, and what a beautiful sight that was.

Her cute little forehead wrinkles smoothed down, her eyes opened wider and looked at him with trust.

She might have even looked at him with love, staring straight through all his bravado as if she could tell that he'd never stopped loving her, either.

He pulled her nearer, and she didn't push away. What fools they'd been. They belonged together; he felt that truth resonate deep within his chest. He, Willow, and Jordyn belonged together. His family.

A woman's piercing scream stopped Ace in his tracks. His eyes tracked the sound to where a dark-haired girl lay on the floor. Then the music stopped, too.

It was Aria. She'd fallen backwards with Jordyn in her arms. Thankfully Jordyn appeared unhurt, but she was shaking like a leaf. She wailed, and Willow ran to her side while Ace checked on Ari. Her breaths came heavily, and her pretty blue eyes rolled backwards.

He dialed 911 with trembling fingers. His heart plummeted when he heard the woman who'd screamed say, "She hit her head, hard." Ace couldn't see any blood, but reported a seizure with potential head trauma to the operator, praying the EMTs could get here as quickly as they did the other day.

He checked his watch. 7 p.m.

Ace spotted Will in the crowd and waved him over. "Can you help me get everyone out of here? There's no rush, if Bo feels like playing another song to soothe everyone's nerves, but I've got to be there for Ari and Willow."

Will's eyes weren't without sympathy, but his face was strained in a strong cry of, "I told you so."

"This is just an emergency." Ace felt a rising panic about the fate of the ranch, but he couldn't think about that now. "I'll be back as quick as I can."

Outside, sirens blared.

Will answered, "I understand, and I can shut down things here. But Ace, I'm done."

"You can't be done."

"I've told you, I'm done with this place. I came out here tonight as a favor to you, but you just roped me back into bailing it out again."

Of all the selfish, short-sighted... couldn't Will see that this was only bad timing, a one-time deal? That Ace hated asking for help? But Will had had enough of Ace's promises and best intentions not to involve anyone else in this money-hole.

Ace didn't have time to go seven rounds with Will. Jordyn was still howling a few feet away. Willow shouldn't have to load a three-year-old in an ambulance by herself. Right then, there was nothing more important than making sure Aria would be okay. Than his family, no longer being by themselves. Even if it cost him the ranch.

9

7:08 p.m. At last, Aria's eyes snapped open in the ambulance. Willow breathed a sigh of relief.

The attending paramedic was the same kindly older lady Willow remembered from their last ride. "How are you feeling, dear?" she asked.

Aria looked around. "Hmm?" She swatted at the oxygen tubing in her nose.

The paramedic gently took Aria's hands, and Willow readjusted Jordyn on her lap. "I thought a seizure wouldn't happen again if she got enough sleep?"

The woman pursed her lips. "I'm not a doctor, but a second seizure in such a short amount of time seems excessive." She laid Ari's hands by her sides, ensured her electrode stickers remained in place for the EKG, and snapped a pulse oximeter on her left finger.

Ace's phone buzzed, and he dismissed the call. Immediately, the call came through again, and he answered it, irritable. "What? I'm on my way to the hospital."

The close quarters enabled everyone on the ambulance to hear Dan Achan's gleeful voice on the other line, even with the sirens blaring outside. "This won't take long. I just wanted you to know that I am the new co-owner of Ernest Ranch. Will sold me his share this evening."

All the color drained from Ace's face. "I'll talk to you later." He hung up.

Fully conscious now, Aria cried, "Ace, I'm so sorry. Is this because of me?"

"Don't you think one minute about it. You've helped me this month more than words can say. The only thing that matters now is you getting well."

He squeezed her cheek lovingly, like he used to do when she was a girl, and Aria's smile returned.

Willow marveled at how Ace had dropped everything again to help Aria, but to abandon his fundraiser? He'd jeopardized the whole ranch for them. She could no longer doubt his commitment, or his priorities.

Now that Aria was awake, Willow called her parents and let them know they were en route to Hoffmann Haven Hospital.

Since Willow's mother had been in town already, she was in the waiting room by the time they breezed Aria through on her stretcher. Riley explained that Patrick was closing up the diner and would join them shortly.

Jordyn's head lolled from side to side on Willow's shoulder. It was so far past her bedtime that even striding through the hospital couldn't keep her awake anymore.

Once they got Aria settled in a room, Riley noticed Jordyn's exhaustion. "Ace, thank you for being here for us." She extended her key ring, which was shaped like a coffee cup. "Would you mind driving Willow and Jordyn home? Patrick and I will get my car from you once things calm down."

"Of course," Ace answered.

"I got a space near the front—you can't miss it."

"Keep us updated, please," Willow said.

"You know we will." Riley pulled her in for a quick hug, and then turned to Aria to brush her sweaty hair away from her face.

"Do you want me to carry Jordyn?" Ace asked as they exited into the hallway.

Willow's arms were burning. "Please."

They paused to gently transfer Jordyn into Ace's embrace. She stirred slightly but didn't wake, and they headed for the parking lot. Seeing Ace gently rub Jordyn's back sent Willow's heart skittering.

"I'm sorry about what happened with Dan. That must really hurt."

"Ah, it's been coming for a long time." He looked everywhere but at her.

Willow peeked over at Ace's eyes, where his bravery didn't quite extend to.

"Will always left his hands off the place, but I'm sure Dan will block me at every turn until I give up my half of the ranch out of sheer frustration." Ace sighed. "I keep asking God for a little more time, but I guess my extensions are up in heaven, too."

Willow tilted her head thoughtfully. "When you've been asking, what do you feel the answer has been?"

Ace looked at her blankly. "The answer? God wants to save the ranch, doesn't he? It's an important place to a lot of people. That's why this doesn't make any sense."

"We can't give up yet. Maybe next time you ask, pause to discern what the answer might be."

Ace frowned. "I feel kind of funny sitting on my knees when I could be getting to work."

There would be no more work to do unless he was able to buy back Will's share and pay his bills, but now wasn't the time for Willow to point that out.

"The Bible says we have to persevere in prayer. That it *is* a kind of work." One she'd become quite familiar with as she agonized over telling Ace her secret. "Maybe God hasn't revealed the answer to you yet, but *you* might feel better if you press in and set aside some time to clear your mind."

"Maybe I'll give it a try." Ace shrugged. "Your ideas have all been great so far."

Willow missed this, talking about God with Ace. He'd been a good person before they got together, but it had been a delight to see his faith grow throughout their relationship.

Though he was newer to the church, Ace had taught Willow many things through his individual background and strengths. How to appreciate the truth instead of being fooled, to not take blessings for granted, and to stand firm when bad things happened.

They found her parents' compact silver car in the front of the lot, as promised. Thankfully, Jordyn had her own car seat there for when she drove around with her grandparents.

Ace passed Jordyn back to Willow so Willow could load her in. She still slept soundly. Willow took the passenger seat, and Ace settled in the driver's seat. In the tiny vehicle, the distance between Willow and tonight's knight in shining armor felt like nothing.

Back to business. Willow started to direct him. "Jordyn and I live in..."

"The apartment complex on the east end of town," Ace finished.

"Have you been keeping tabs on me?" Willow asked, secretly delighted at the thought.

Ace lifted his right shoulder. "Bo shares some news, from time to time. Honestly, I didn't like when he did, but that was only because I missed you so much."

Ace reversed the car, his eyes fully focused on the road behind him, but something about the darkness of the hour loosened Willow's lips.

"I missed you, too," she whispered.

"Even if the ranch goes under, I hope I'll still be seeing you around." Ace swallowed hard, though his tone was casual, as if this were the most normal conversation in the world.

"You will."

Ace watched Jordyn and Willow climb the whitewashed exterior stairway of their apartment complex and safely disappear into their home. This was their everyday reality, but it felt wrong to leave them there now. Witnessing how Willow and Jordyn lived alone was much more unsettling than simply knowing that fact in theory.

Before he turned the car towards home, for the first time in four years, Ace found himself driving to church.

It was abandoned, of course, the late hour leaving a sacred hush over the grassy parking lot. The lawn needed mowing. That was something he used to keep an eye on when he attended.

Ace rolled to a stop and cut the engine. There was nobody around. He was far from Sommerton, where a ton of cleanup work from the fundraiser awaited him. But now? It was just him and the Lord.

"Father," he began. His first thought was, "Please save the ranch.

Please." But he took Willow's advice and slowed down his words. "My heart's broken. Dan is taking my dream away. I know that sounds selfish, but what'll happen to the horses? To all the kids in riding lessons? To Bo? I'm sorry I let everyone down. I've come to the end of myself and what I'm able to do."

Ace hung his head on the steering wheel, emptied out mentally and emotionally. Then, he thought he heard an answer, stirring up his heart like a gentle breeze: *I will provide.*

Ace looked to the starry sky through his windshield. "Provide what? And when?"

I will provide, again resounded in Ace's mind.

How could God expect him to let go of the details when anything could happen?

Ace took in a cleansing breath. Holding onto the ranch so tightly had thus far caused him nothing but trouble. He'd still lost Will's share, despite all his striving, and it had cost him the past four years with Willow.

"I surrender to You, Lord," Ace's words dispelled the weight of his worries. "I'm sorry I've been so far away."

But Ace felt no condemnation. Only the comforting hand of a Father's touch. The thing he'd always needed most in the world.

He could look at his problems with fresh eyes tomorrow. For now, for once, Ace needed to rest.

10

In a group text which included him and Willow, Ace received updates on Aria from Riley all through Saturday night. Apparently, the doctor on duty couldn't push aside their concerns this time. On-site, they made an appointment with a neurological specialist in St. Louis, and Aria had to follow a special diet in the meantime.

Since Aria had been cleared for discharge tonight, Wednesday evening, Ace figured the text that came through was the announcement that Aria was headed home, but instead, it was from Willow, asking if she could swing by the ranch the following evening after work.

Sure, he replied. Maybe she was coming by to pick up the sound system.

Bo and Will had cleaned up all the decorations and put them back in Willow's bins, so there wasn't much left for Ace to deconstruct. He just kept busy with his normal chores and took some time to read a few chapters in Genesis.

Thursday, the grind of outdoor repair work at the railroad made the day pass quickly. Ace was back at the ranch by six and barely had time to wipe his grimy face before Willow knocked on his office door.

He opened it in a half-second. "Hey. How are you?" She looked exhausted.

"Good." She looked antsy, too, like a racer waiting for the starting gun. He gestured for her to sit. "I have another idea," she said.

"Okay." Ace drew out the word's two syllables, unsure what she was about to say. He was open to suggestions but couldn't see a way out of his predicament.

"Just promise you won't say anything until I'm through with my pitch."

He smiled. "A true businesswoman. All right, I promise."

"Bo and I wrote another song today, to raise awareness for the cause, while the rest of the class watched a musical. Our creative spirits took over, and we finished within the hour. We call it 'Earnest Ace.'" She gave him a timid smile. "Thought that was a nice play on words."

A song with his name in it? This couldn't be good.

She closed her eyes, and her voice put him at ease for a moment.

A little boy,
Screamed at, neglected.
Never expected
Somethin' good.

The moment was over. She hadn't sung anything untrue, but he felt exposed when she laid out his past like that. Her intense eyes opened then, as if reminding him what he'd just agreed to.

Meets a gentle man
With seven steady horses
That reached a wild heart
Like no one could.

That verse was surely about Wyatt Ernest. Willow extended her palm to show the next part would be about Ace.

He's a hero.
He's survived the worst.
And he turned that to a blessing
Not a curse.

He's a hero.

68

See him standing strong.
Won't leave them all alone
When they've found a home.

He worked two jobs
To take care of others.
But who takes care of him?
Lost his big brother.

Now he's crying out,
Hoping for a sunrise.
For people to care
And open their eyes.

He's a hero.
He's survived the worst.
And he turned that to a blessing
Not a curse.

He's a hero.
See him standing strong.
Won't leave them all alone
When they've found a home.

Willow looked at him hopefully. Not only that, but with admiration. Ace didn't want to deny her anything after she bore out her heart like that. But as she bared her heart, she also revealed some very personal details about him.

"I'm honored that this is how you feel about me, Willow. But I don't know if you can sing that for anyone else. Wouldn't it seem self-promoting?"

"People need to know the man behind the ranch. How much you care for this place, and how much you've sacrificed for it. No one will ever accuse you of trying to make a celebrity out of yourself."

He shifted his position in his folding chair. "I also don't want to hurt Will's feelings with the line about the brother."

"Bo actually wrote that part. Will was wrong, Ace."

"The way Will sees it, I turned my back on him by saddling him with the ranch's problems again."

"For Aria! He'll come around." Willow crossed her arms jauntily.

"You're unstoppable, like a bull out of a gate. But your heart's in the right place."

"There's more to gain than to lose by putting this song out there. I think you'll truly touch people, like you have Bo and me."

Ace threw his arms up in the air. "Fine. How many people will actually hear it, anyway?"

Willow clapped her hands. "Only the entire internet. Plus, the radio station agreed to give it a spin if we record in their studio. Aria will make us a cute cover. I've still got pictures of you in that old hat."

He groaned. "I don't want to know any more. Just do it."

Willow gave him a hug, then all thoughts of her plans evaporated. There was just her sugar-sweet perfume. Her words of encouragement still ringing in his ears. He leaned in, slowly enough to let her stop him if that's what she wanted.

She grabbed a fistful of his shirt and kissed him soundly. He'd forgotten the strength of her warmth, the feel of her silky hair and her soft arms. It gave him the urge to protect her and love her with everything he had. He never wanted this moment to end.

But end it did. Willow pulled back and put her hand over her mouth. "I don't know what came over me."

"Can it come over you again?" Ace asked hazily.

"I don't think that would be the best idea. You'd better ask me out on a proper date, or we'll be here all day, making up for lost time."

His heart revved like a racecar engine at the thought of taking Willow out. He'd hardly believed they'd get another chance. Maybe miracles could happen after all.

Willow thought about their kiss all week long, even as busy as she was teaching, spending time with Jordyn, and recording "Earnest Ace." The DJ insisted they got a good, clean take and edited the audio file within a day. Aria, not to be tied down by her recent emergency room visit, designed the cover in short order, and before long, "Earnest Ace" was available on every major music distribution avenue they could access for free, captioned with a plea to donate.

In the middle of all the chaos, there were a few stolen moments where Willow recalled the feel of Ace holding her close, marveling at how their connection hadn't ended over time. They'd been texting back and forth about the song's progress, with a smidgen of flirtation thrown in.

By the time she and Jordyn drove out to the ranch to deliver Aria to her Saturday volunteer shift, Willow had heard their song on the radio every hour for a week. The DJ had come through beyond the obligation of the nominal fee they'd paid him, frequently encouraging listeners to contribute to the cause, even if it was just a few dollars. The community had responded with open arms, requesting constant replays and calling in with stories about their visit to the ranch.

Aria, Bo, and Ace were busier than ever, with an influx of new weekend visitors. Ace's finances were inching out of the red. But could the ranch's sudden popularity be enough to support the horses for the long run?

Today, Willow decided she and Jordyn would go say hi to Ace before heading back home and maybe spend some time there. In the parking lot, they crossed paths with a man dressed much more finely than they were accustomed to seeing at the ranch. He was wearing a soft periwinkle cashmere sweater and pressed pants. He nodded cordially before getting into a sleek luxury car.

Jordyn, who was becoming more familiar with the ranch, ran straight to the Shetland ponies' stalls, while Aria wandered away to start feeding duty. Willow caught up with her daughter and had just extended her hand to pat Pinky's neck when strong arms wrapped her from behind.

Willow started, turned, and slapped Ace's shoulder playfully. "Haven't you grown out of that yet?"

"Never have. Never will."

She rolled her eyes.

"I'm glad you're here. Did you see the man that just left?"

"The rich one?" she said frankly.

"Don't you know who that was?" Ace sighed. "All those hours of watching the Kentucky Derby tapings with me, and you learned nothing."

"Your fault, I'm sure. You always distracted me from the show."

"No, I remember now. You found it boring and would scribble down song lyrics or do your homework instead of appreciating the sport's beauty. Never mind. The point is that he's Allen Fuller!" Ace splayed out his fingers in a ta-da motion that had no effect on Willow's memory whatsoever.

"Who?"

He sighed again. "The retired jockey who holds the all-time record of six championship wins? The Missouri native?" Ace clasped Willow's hands.

"He says he wants to help with the ranch. He heard your song. The first horse he ever trained on was a rescue, and he wanted to know why the ranch is in trouble. He said he'd invest enough so that I could come on full-time and repair the damage from the fire. He said he may be able to get some of his friends interested in investing, too."

"That's amazing!" Willow bit her lip. "What about Dan, though? Won't he still spoil everything?"

"Excuse me?" Oliver Achan had entered the property. Talk about awkward timing.

Willow started, "About what I said just now. I know Dan's your son, but..."

Oliver waved away her protests. "You don't have to say anything more. I know how Dan is, and that's why I'm here." He sighed deeply and spoke now to Ace. "I owe you an apology. You see, the night of the fire on your ranch, Dan was with me, but only at the end of the evening. Covered in sweat and smelling like smoke."

He covered his face with wrinkled hands. "I should have told the police the truth, but instead I let Dan shower it off, and I lied about what time he arrived. Willow's dad has been questioning me for weeks, wrecking my peaceful Monday night burgers. But I couldn't keep it a secret anymore, not once I heard that song on the radio. Even after I shut it off, it just kept playing in my mind, how my son made you lose everything, and it just wasn't right." Oliver looked up then. "We'll help you pay for the damages. If you still want to press charges, I understand."

Ace stepped back and crossed his arms. "If the damages are paid for, and Dan agrees to give up his claim to the ranch and stop all this sabotage, we have a deal. I don't need to see him behind bars. All I've ever wanted was for him to leave this place alone."

"Thank you. I'll talk sense into him, I promise." The elderly man lumbered away. He was a good person. Willow felt sorry that he had ended up with such a bad apple of a son, but perhaps this would be a lesson learned for them both.

Ace swept her close again. "How's that for answered prayers?"

"I'd say that God's made a way for us again."

They pivoted back towards their daughter, soaking in her talking to "her pony" with joy, gratitude, and joined hands.

Three months later, Willow married Ace amidst bouquets of bluebells at their church. Jordyn had been delighted to learn that her mommy and daddy were romantically involved, and they decided they had been apart long enough.

Willow and Jordyn commuted to Hoffmann Haven on weekdays from Ace's little farmhouse, which was filled with love and lots of rasta pasta, this time cooked in a proper pot. Willow dropped Jordyn off each morning to Riley at Golden Days, where Aria was thriving and even had gained her own low-carb, low-glycemic section on the diner menu. Unless, of course, Jordyn decided to be a farm girl for the day with Daddy, soaking up the sunshine and running wild.

Even with the longer drive to work, Willow felt the pressure of doing it all on her own melt away. Weekends were busy but full of life as the community events at Ernest Ranch continued, stretching Willow's imagination to use different themes and activities to delight their neighbors.

Yes, the rancher had found his reason to make his business better than it ever had been before—his lovely wife and their little angel girl —united together enjoying God's daily, and sometimes unexpected, blessings.

THE END

Acknowledgements

Thanks be to God, who gave me this story suddenly and forcefully when I said I wouldn't write any more books. It's been fun to see all the groundwork snap into place.

To all the women I know who make the world a more beautiful place with their hearts and ingenuity. To all the men I know who give and forgive courageously. To all the children I know who teach adults how to live with joy and color. Never forget your value to God. I hope these characters pay tribute to these everyday miracles.

Mom, your proofreading advice and excitement is always of great benefit. Savanna for lifting me up and helping my stories come alive. Sofie, Julie, and Tori, thank you for your contributions to the beautiful cover. Thank you Mike, for your faithfulness in keeping my website up to date. Belen and Sofie-thanks for going line dancing with me. I'm also grateful to Grammy and my family for supporting my continual ranch-going efforts!

Thank you to Kerry for sharing your ideas and encouragement during the initial brainstorming stage. Laura, thank you for sharing your thoughts on each chapter. To the small business owners and new friends in my community. Your creativity and support amaze me!

Thank you, reader, for taking the time to read my story! It means so much whenever I see your review or hear that you enjoyed the book.

May God's blessings shine forth on your life!

About the Author

Rachel Blanchard is a teacher, wife, and mother of three young children. She loves frequenting theme parks and bookstores in sunny Central Florida! She is passionate about sharing lessons learned, and the message that we can trust in God's goodness.

Also Available from Rachel Blanchard

Small-Town Romances
First in My Heart
Finding My Heart

Medieval Fantasy
Cassia's Calling